The SEVENTH TOWER

ABOVE THE VEIL

THE SEVENTH TOWER

ABOVE THE VEIL

GARTH NIX

HarperCollins *Children's Books*

First published in the USA by Scholastic Inc 2001
First published in Great Britain by HarperCollins *Children's Books* 2009
HarperCollins *Children's Books* is a division of HarperCollins*Publishers* Ltd,
77-85 Fulham Palace Road, Hammersmith, London W6 8JB

www.harpercollins.co.uk

www.garthnix.co.uk

3

ISBN 978 0 00 726122 2

Printed and bound in England by
Clays Ltd, St Ives plc

Mixed Sources
Product group from well-managed
forests and other controlled sources
www.fsc.org Cert no. SW-COC-1806
© 1996 Forest Stewardship Council

FSC is a non-profit international organisation established to promote the
responsible management of the world's forests. Products carrying the FSC
label are independently certified to assure consumers that they come
from forests that are managed to meet the social, economic and
ecological needs of present and future generations.

Find out more about HarperCollins and the environment at
www.harpercollins.co.uk/green

To the total Seventh Tower team:
All the people at Scholastic and Lucasfilm
who have worked so hard on publishing
the books and getting them to readers.

1

The Chosen rarely entered the Underfolk levels of the Castle. As long as their servants continued to work, they ignored them. Long ago there had been Chosen overseers who regularly inspected all seven Underfolk levels and even the odd chambers and workrooms below the lowest level. But in the past hundred years or more, only the occasional adult Chosen would wander through, though bands of Chosen children would sometimes explore for a few hours.

All that changed in a moment. Without warning, scores of Chosen were spreading out across the seventh and lowest of the Underfolk levels. Most of them wore the gold Sunstone-set bracers of the Empress's Guard and held naked swords in their hands.

As they pushed open doors and ran down corridors, their shouts filled the air and their Spiritshadows flickered across every floor and wall. Sunstones flashed brightly, illuminating dark corners and possible hiding places. If anything moved, the light was followed by bolts of incandescence that incinerated caveroaches, rats and whatever else fled from their intensive search.

The Underfolk stopped and stood still as stone while the hunting parties of Chosen scoured their workrooms and caverns. They knew that this was the safest thing to do. But not all Underfolk realised the danger, or were quick enough to stop and identify themselves. One old, very deaf woman did not hear the command to stop as she limped along a dimly lit corridor. The guard did not shout twice, but followed the command with a Red Ray of Destruction from his Sunstone.

When the body was revealed to be an old woman – not one of the fugitives the guards sought – there was no apology or explanation. The guards simply moved away, their needle-waisted Spiritshadows sliding after them. The body, like everything else destroyed, ruined or discarded by the Chosen, would be cleaned up by the Underfolk.

In the chamber where the Castle's fifty-six level laundry chute ended, the Chosen in charge of this unprecedented search of the Underfolk levels sat at ease on a pile of laundry bags, eating dried shrimps from a pocket in his sleeve.

At first sight he seemed like a normal Chosen. His Sunstones and glowing staff declared him to be a Brightblinder, the Deputy Lumenor of the Orange Order, and a Shadowmaster of the Empress. His face was plump and his mouth was small and cruel, but he was otherwise undistinguished.

His Spiritshadow was more imposing. A thing of spikes and sharp edges, it was taller than a man. Its head bore two horns and, in addition to a mouth of many fangs, it had four upper limbs that each ended in a cluster of hooked claws. It stood upright on two lesser-clawed legs and paced behind its master's seat of laundry bags, as if it cared more about the objects of this search than its master. In the light of so many Sunstones, it almost seemed to be made of solid, jet-black flesh, rather than shadow.

The fat, shrimp-eating man was not a normal Chosen. He gave orders to the guards as they came and went, and all of them were Chosen of higher Order and rank. There were Chosen of the Blue, Indigo and Violet, but all bowed their heads before this Orange Chosen and gave a respectful flash of light from their Sunstones.

Most bowed low enough that they did not have to look at the gaping wound in his chest, a ghastly fist-sized hole that they could see right through, from front to back. The hole did not bleed and this strange Chosen showed no discomfort from it, though the Merwin-horn sword that had punched so easily through bone and flesh had been withdrawn less than an hour before.

That sword lay at his feet now, gently glowing. There was no blood on it.

Shadowmaster Sushin settled further back on his makeshift seat and ate the last of the shrimps. Then he rubbed his hands on a Yellow robe that was poking out the top of one of the laundry bags and looked at the latest guard who had come back to report – a Shadowlord of the Violet.

"We've lost them," said the guard, her head bowed. "They went into a belish root forest and disappeared. We're clearing the roots, but there is no sign of them."

The guard's Spiritshadow shrank back as its mistress spoke, so that it almost hid behind her, though its broad shoulders were wider than any human's by at least a stretch.

Sushin frowned.

"Keep searching, Ethar," he said. "Make sure the Underfolk understand that they are to report any sign of the fugitives. I am returning upward to attend to... other matters. Remember, I want them both dead and the bodies and clothing destroyed. But their Sunstones are to be returned to me. That is most important. We must not risk losing their Sunstones."

Ethar looked up, straight at the hole in Sushin's chest. She seemed about to speak, but Sushin stopped her. He raised his hand, displaying a particularly large and vibrant Sunstone ring that shone with the purest Violet, dimming the light from the other rings on his hand.

"Do you question my orders, Shadowlord – or my authority?"

Ethar stared for a second longer, then looked away.

"No, Sushin," she said finally. "I know with whose voice you speak."

She turned away and gestured to the guards who were keeping a respectful distance. As they left, Sushin chuckled and mumbled something too soft for Ethar to hear.

"Do you, Ethar? Do you really?"

"No, you push the lever in and turn it at the same time," said Tal as Adras, his Spiritshadow, once again pawed ineffectually at the handle of the hatch. "Look, I'll do it."

He started to climb back, but Adras finally managed to work the handle out. The hatch shut behind them.

"Now I want you to twist the handle off," said Tal. There wasn't any lock on the hatch, but if Adras pulled the handle off, it might jam the mechanism. Nobody would be able to follow them down.

"Need light," Adras puffed as he wrenched at the handle. "Not strong enough."

Tal made sure his foothold was secure before extending his hand. The Sunstone set in the ring he wore flashed orange and then turned to white, steadily growing brighter and brighter.

With the light, Adras became more clearly defined. A Storm Shepherd from the spirit world of Aenir, here on the Dark World he was a free Spiritshadow, bound to be with Tal, but not necessarily to obey him. It was a situation Tal regretted most of the time.

The billowing cloud of shadow was vaguely manlike, but twice the size of Tal. One mighty arm heaved and the lever broke off in his hands. He was about to drop it when Tal shouted.

"No! Pass it to me! Milla and Odris are below us, remember?"

"Sorry," Adras said as he passed the broken lever to Tal. Tal put it in his pocket, sighed and recommenced his downward climb.

Tal had found the hatch only by accident, stubbing his toe on the lip as they raced through one of the vast caverns where the Underfolk cultivated thousands of ugly strings of the root vegetable they called belish. Tal had never liked eating belish and pushing through a thick forest of muddy belish roots wasn't much fun either. But the accidental discovery of the hatch had made it all worthwhile. The guards had been closing in.

Now Tal was in a narrow tube leading down at a forty-five-degree angle. There was no proper ladder, but spikes had been driven into the stone close enough together to use as foot- and handholds. There was no permanent light either, no Sunstones set in the walls, floor or ceiling. To get light, Tal pointed his Sunstone down and an answering light flashed back up from Milla's Sunstone, twin to his own.

Milla was descending quickly, wasting no time. The Icecarl girl was now totally focused on leaving the Castle and returning to the ice. She believed that she had made wrong decisions and sailed a wrong course. The Spiritshadow at her side was a constant reminder of her pride and failure. Only on the ice could she atone for her misdeeds.

That Spiritshadow followed her now. Like Adras, Odris had been a Storm Shepherd less than a day before, but that had been in the spirit world of Aenir. Here in the Dark World she was Milla's Spiritshadow – and having a Spiritshadow was against every Icecarl rule and custom.

Milla believed the loss of her ordinary shadow meant the end of her dream to be a Shield Maiden... and probably the end of her life as well. Only the need to inform the Crones about what was going on in the Castle and Aenir would prevent her from giving herself to the Ice as soon as she got out of the Castle.

But first they all had to get away from Sushin and the guards. Then they had to find Tal's great-uncle Ebbitt and try to make sense of everything they'd learned. Not that Ebbitt was ever much help in making sense of things, Tal thought. But he might be able to explain what the Keystones were, how they controlled the Veil and how Tal's father, Rerem, could be affected by the Orange Keystone... What was it the Codex had said?

He is the Guardian of the Orange Keystone. It has been unsealed and so he does not live. Until or unless the Orange Keystone is sealed again, he does not live. If it is sealed, he will live again.

There was also Gref – Tal's brother – to think about. Tal had almost rescued him, but was foiled at the last moment by Sushin's tricks. Gref had been poisoned or somehow put into a coma. Just like Tal's mother, Graile... though she had been sick for a long time.

Tal had tried so hard to help his family, to live up to his father's wish that he look after them. But whatever he did, something always went wrong. In the beginning he thought all he had to do was get a new Sunstone, and that was hard enough.

Life was a *lot* harder now.

Distracted by these thoughts, Tal didn't hear Milla call out to him from down below, until his Spiritshadow tapped him quite hard on the head.

"Ow!"

"Milla says there's a drop into water," Adras reported, his voice too loud as usual. Even as a Spiritshadow, he retained the characteristics of a Storm Shepherd. He boomed rather than spoke, and shadow-lightning crackled around his eyes and fingers.

Tal looked down, shining his Sunstone. Milla had stopped and was shining her Sunstone further into the tunnel. Something reflected back, quite a long way from them. What water could it be? Tal frowned, trying to remember long-ago lessons about the layout of the Castle.

They were climbing down from the seventh Underfolk level, which was filled with various workrooms, vegetable and fungus farms, and manufactories. The seventh was the lowest complete Underfolk level, except for some isolated forges and... the fish pools.

That was what lay underneath them. One of the huge pools where the Underfolk farmed fish. Yellowscale and finners for the Chosen's tables, and the translucent shrimps that were such a delicacy when dried. Sometimes there were eels in the ponds too, but they were considered vermin by the Chosen, left to the Underfolk to eat.

"It's shallow!" Tal shouted down to Milla. "Don't jump."

Milla scowled back at him and jumped anyway.

But she jumped holding on to Odris. Even as

Spiritshadows, the Storm Shepherds retained some of their cloud characteristics. Milla floated like a feather, with Odris spread out in a great billow of darkness above her.

Milla splashed down gently, the water only up to her waist. She raised her hand and increased the light from her Sunstone. She hadn't had the stone very long, but Tal noticed she was rapidly gaining better control of it, even though he'd given her only the briefest of lessons. He found this unsettling. Only the Chosen were supposed to be able to use Sunstones.

It was yet another part of his world and his beliefs that had started to come apart at the seams. Tal wasn't sure what was true any more. Most of what he'd been taught in the Lectorium seemed to be half-truths or only part of the whole picture. It was almost as if the main purpose of his schooling had been to blind him to wider knowledge, rather than teach him.

"Come on!" Milla ordered.

Tal sighed and climbed down to the last spike, then reached up to take Adras's hand. The

Spiritshadow accepted it absently and let go just as Tal was about to drop.

"Hold on to me!" Tal said. "And you need to puff up, so we can float down."

"Sorry," boomed Adras. "I was thinking about home."

"Well, don't," Tal muttered.

This time the Spiritshadow did as he was told, hanging on to Tal and puffing up so they made a controlled descent.

Even so, Tal cried out as they hit the water. In the dash to escape, he'd momentarily forgotten the pain from the Waspwyrm sting. The jar of landing and the cool water sent a jab of pain right through him, and he stumbled forward, almost sinking underwater.

Adras hauled him up, and Milla and Odris looked around.

"Are you all right?" Odris asked. Characteristically, Milla didn't say anything. Tal knew that she would never have cried out from something as simple as pain. He gritted his teeth and stood upright, wincing as his leg spasmed.

"I'm fine," he said, though it took an effort to speak. "Let's go."

"Where?" asked Milla. She held her Sunstone ring high so that its light spread out all around them, illuminating a wide circle of shimmering water. Beyond that circle was darkness.

Tal turned his head, looking all around. The fish ponds were extremely large, he knew, some of them two or three thousand stretches in diameter. But there would be a dock or platform somewhere, so the fish, once caught, could be boxed and transported up to the storehouses and kitchens.

The only problem was knowing in which direction that dock lay.

"Douse your light," Milla said suddenly. She stared at her Sunstone ring. When the light did not fade fast enough, she covered it with her other hand. Tal, who was properly trained, made his wink out in a second.

"Why?" Tal whispered as they stood in the darkness. For some reason the whole cavern seemed much quieter without light and he didn't want to disturb that silence.

Milla's only answer was a slight splashing sound. She was moving around.

"I don't like this," said Adras. "I feel weak."

"I feel sick," said Odris. "Like being thirsty back on Aenir."

"It's only for a moment," Milla told them. Her voice

startled Tal, coming from behind him and further out than he expected. "Ah, I have it now."

Light flared on her hand again. Tal let his Sunstone surge in answer.

"Have what?" he asked.

"There is light over there," said Milla, pointing. "And I heard something too. But it is distant. This cavern... this fish pond... is very large."

"It could be the biggest one," said Tal. "There are three I think."

Vague and unpleasant memories of childhood tales were coming back to him. Something about the big fish pond and enormous eels, each ten stretches long and with an appetite to match.

He remembered laughing as a child at the thought of Underfolk being surprised by a giant eel. It didn't seem so funny now that *he* was wading in the fish pond.

Something brushed his waist and Tal yelped and leapt back. In that same second, he recognised what it was. A weed. A thick black rope of seaweed, with huge bulbous air nodes that kept it floating on the surface.

Milla lifted up a strand. "This is different from the seaweeds we harvest under the Ice. I don't think this can be eaten."

"Definitely not," said Tal, grimacing in distaste. He pushed the weed away. It was slimy, it smelled bad – and there was a lot more of it to wade through.

As Tal moved the weed away, he saw a face in the water. He almost flinched as he saw it, thinking someone else was creeping up behind him, before he realised who it was.

It was his own reflection, but so different from the last time he'd looked in a proper mirror that he almost didn't recognise himself. That had been only a few weeks before, but so much had happened.

The young Chosen boy with the slightly scraggly dark brown hair and lopsided smile was gone. In his place there was someone Tal would have once described as a wild man. His hair was crazier and dirtier, and there was a broad stripe down the middle that was bright green, the result of an encounter with a monster in Aenir. His face appeared to be permanently set in a tense expression that was half scowl and half frown. He looked quite a lot older than his almost fourteen years.

"Come on," said Milla.

Tal realised he'd been staring at his reflection. He looked across at Milla and noticed that she had changed too. She had discarded her temporary disguise of a Chosen matron's Yellow robe, and openly wore her Icecarl furs and Selski-hide armour. She still had her white-blonde hair tied back. But something had changed.

It took him a moment to realise that the change was in her green eyes. The fierceness had gone out of them, as if some spark had been lost.

Only then did Tal understand that she really was going to give herself to the Ice. When he'd thought he was saving her life – and his own – by agreeing to take the two Storm Shepherds as Spiritshadows, he had only postponed Milla's fate. She would take her own life because she had lost her own shadow and gained a Spiritshadow instead.

"Come on!" Milla repeated. She started wading off through the water, pausing every now and then to push apart particularly difficult strands of the bulbous seaweed.

Tal followed more slowly. He felt incredibly tired all of a sudden. Everything felt like it was too hard. No matter what he did, he made things worse. Now he knew he had to make sure Milla survived. The only way he could think of doing that was to stop her leaving the Castle, which would be totally against her wishes. And going against Milla's wishes was almost never a good idea.

Perhaps Ebbitt would be able to figure something out, Tal thought wearily.

Ebbitt. They had to find Ebbitt – wherever he was – before the guards caught up with them.

Or caught up with Ebbitt, Tal suddenly thought. That hadn't occurred to him before.

He groaned. Milla, Adras and Odris all stopped and looked at him.

"What is it?" Milla asked. She already had her bone knife in her hand, drawn in an instant.

Tal shook his head.

"Nothing. I just realised how stupid this is. We're looking for Ebbitt, but we don't know where he is or what we can do once we find him. There are guards everywhere, not to mention Sushin, whatever in Light's name *he* actually is. We're in a scum-filled fish pond. I haven't done anything right and I don't understand what's going on..."

His voice trailed off as Milla stared at him. It was not the Icecarl way to complain, he knew. It was the Chosen way though. Chosen complained about Underfolk servants, about food quality, about their clothes, about anything.

Anything trivial, Tal thought. Did he really want to be like that?

He looked down at his reflection again and tried to force a smile. It came slowly and for some reason it no longer had that annoying crooked curve on the left side.

"On the other hand," he said slowly, "I have a new Sunstone, which is all I wanted to start with. And a Spiritshadow—"

"That's me," said Adras proudly.

"And we have the Codex hidden up in the Mausoleum," Tal continued. Saying the positive things made him feel a bit better about the whole situation. "So what am I complaining about?"

"I don't know," said Milla. She frowned and added, "You are alive. Be grateful for the gift of life, till you have it no more."

She turned and ploughed off through the weed again, faster than before. Tal followed, wincing at the pain in his leg. She was going faster than was comfortable for him, but he didn't complain.

It was hard going, wading through the seaweed. There was a lot more of it than Tal would have thought was healthy for a working fish pond. For that matter, there didn't seem to be any fish. Or eels. Though it was possible they had scared the fish away, or couldn't see them in the dark. Milla had insisted that they keep their Sunstones down to dim sparks so they didn't give themselves away. Adras and Odris had complained at first, but seemed to have got used to feeling weak from the lack of light.

Tal waded for at least fifteen minutes without a single thought and without being aware of what he was doing. He just pushed through the seaweed, following Milla. He would have mindlessly kept on doing it too, except she stopped.

"What is it?" he whispered, edging around her.

"Look," Milla whispered back.

Tal looked. There was some light ahead. But it wasn't the clear, steady illumination of Sunstones. The light was flickering and fairly weak, changing colour quite a bit. A couple of oil lamps, Tal thought – the ones the Underfolk used in the parts of the Castle where there were no fixed Sunstones. Underfolk couldn't use Sunstones of course, so they had to make do with oil lanterns and similar devices.

In the dim light, Tal could see four... no... five people hard at work. Two were in the water, passing loads of something up, while the others were taking whatever it was and putting it in barrels.

"Underfolk harvesting fish," Tal said, not bothering to keep his voice down. "We can just walk past—"

A cold hand across his mouth cut him off.

"Quiet," Milla whispered fiercely. "They're not normal Underfolk. And they're not harvesting fish."

For a moment Tal was tempted to bite her hand, but the moment passed and Milla took her hand away. Besides, as he squinted at the dock, he realised there was something funny about these Underfolk. They weren't wearing regular white robes, for a start. And they weren't harvesting fish. It was the seaweed they were dragging up, cutting it into lengths on the dock before putting it in the barrels.

"They have spears," said Milla quietly. Her eyesight was much better than Tal's, particularly in the dark or near-dark. "And one of them has a long knife. Ah—"

One of them had stopped exactly where the lantern light fell most brightly. He was a boy not much older than Tal, but taller and more muscular. He wore Underfolk whites, but something had been painted or embroidered on the cloth – some sort of pattern or writing that Tal couldn't make out from a distance. He also wore a strange triangular hat, with the sharpest peak at the front. It had several long black or deep blue feathers stuck to it at a jaunty angle.

He looked vaguely familiar. Tal felt sure he'd seen him somewhere before, but he couldn't work out where.

Milla could though.

"It is the one called Crow," she said. "The leader of

the people who brought us up from the heatways, when the air went bad."

"Them?" asked Tal. He'd been partially unconscious, or delirious, from the fumes in the heatway tunnels. If they hadn't been rescued, they would have died down there. He hadn't had time to think about the people who'd carried them out. Now it was all coming back.

"Yes," said Milla. "We had better be careful. Most of them wanted to kill us. And they hate the Chosen."

"What?" asked Tal. "They're Underfolk! They can't hate the Chosen! It's... it's not allowed."

"They are not normal Underfolk. It is like I said before. They are Outcasts."

Tal stared at the Underfolk. It was true they were wearing very odd clothes. And no Underfolk had any business to be in the heatway tunnels, where they'd rescued Tal and Milla. He had heard that some Underfolk rebelled against the Chosen and lived below the normal levels. But he'd never really believed it.

"There are only five of them," he said finally. "We both have Sunstones, and Adras and Odris."

"But we're weak," said Odris, a plaintive voice in the darkness. "I couldn't crush a caveroach the way I feel at the moment."

"I could," Adras chimed in. "I could easily crush a caveroach and maybe something about as big as a Dattu or, say, a Lowock—"

"I was *exaggerating*," interrupted Odris. "Of course I could crush a *caveroach*. But I wouldn't be much use in a proper fight—"

"I would be," Adras said proudly. "But if there was more light—"

"Quiet, both of you," Milla ordered.

"We have to get past them," said Tal. "There's no other way out of this lake. And the guards will probably find that trapdoor soon."

"We owe them life," said Milla, the words coming out slowly as if she were thinking aloud. "That means we must talk to them first. They may know where to find your greatest uncle Ebbitt."

"*Great*-uncle, not *greatest*," Tal corrected. "I doubt it though. Underfolk don't normally know anything except their jobs. I wonder what they're planning to do with that weed?"

"Adras, Odris, be prepared to defend us if they attack," said Milla. "We'll give you more light. Let's go."

They were only a dozen stretches from the dock when the Underfolk noticed them. It was Crow who glanced across the water, alerted by a splash. Shock flicked across his face, but it was gone in an instant as he shouted and grabbed his spear.

"Look out! In the water!"

The other two Underfolk on the dock went for their spears as well, while the two in the water splashed in a panic to the steps. Weed went flying through the air as the Underfolk threw it aside in their haste to get weapons or get out of the water.

"Peace!" shouted Milla. "A truce!"

"Talk!" shouted Tal. "We just want to talk!"

Unfortunately, Adras decided at the same moment that he would help with a thunder shout. It broke across the water with all the strength of real thunder, drowning out everyone's words and momentarily stunning the Underfolk.

As the thunder echoed through the pool, Crow threw his spear straight at Tal. Milla leapt forward and snatched it out of the air.

Tal fell into the water, up to his neck. But he kept his hand and Sunstone ring above the surface. Suddenly angry, all his thoughts focused on bringing forth blinding brilliance.

Light exploded out of the stone, banishing the darkness. Adras and Odris roared with delight, suddenly visible as hard-edged shadows, huge humanlike figures of billowing cloud. They rushed at the other Underfolk, who threw their spears uselessly at the Spiritshadows. Adras and Odris batted them away.

It looked like a full-scale battle was about to develop when Milla shouted, using the voice that she had been trained to use aboard an iceship at the height of a gale.

"Stop! Everybody stop!"

Everybody stopped. They might have started again if Milla hadn't kept on shouting.

"Adras! Odris! Come back here. You Underfolk, stay where you are. We just want to talk! We're not Chosen!"

Tal dragged himself up from the water, pushing the weed off his shoulders. He kept his Sunstone burning bright, but deflected the light off the distant ceiling so it didn't blind anybody.

"It's them," said one of the Underfolk, a tall blond-haired boy... no... girl who Tal suddenly remembered was called Gill. "The two we dragged up from adit three. I told you we should have killed them."

"Close it," said Crow. He was looking at Tal and Milla, but his eyes kept shooting across at Adras and Odris. He had a knife in his hand, held low at his side.

"We aren't Chosen," repeated Milla. She ignored Tal's furious look at her. She might not be Chosen, but he was and he couldn't see any point in pretending otherwise.

"No?" asked Crow. "You have Sunstones and Spiritshadows."

"I am Milla, an Icecarl, from outside the Castle. Tal... used to be a Chosen, but he's not any more. The Chosen have cast him out. The guards are after him."

Tal opened his mouth to protest, then shut it again. Milla was describing what had happened to him in her terms, but it was still true. He was effectively an Outcast. He hadn't really thought it through before.

Crow listened without changing his expression. Even the news that Milla came from outside the Castle didn't seem to perturb him. The others shifted nervously and looked behind them to the open door and the tunnel beyond.

"We're looking for my great-uncle Ebbitt," said Tal. "An old Chosen. His Spiritshadow has the shape of a maned cat. Have you seen him down here?"

"Maybe," said Crow. Tal noticed that the other Underfolk seemed to recognise Ebbitt's name and they wouldn't meet his eyes. It was also clear Crow was their leader and they would stand silently while he did the talking.

"Can you take us to him?" asked Milla.

"That depends, doesn't it?" said Crow.

"On what?" Tal asked. He was getting more and more angry. "Why don't you... why don't you just do as you're told?"

Even as the words left his mouth, Tal regretted them. This was exactly how he'd got in trouble with the Icecarls. His mind knew better, but it was slower than his tongue.

Crow stared at him, his dark eyes shining with a deep hatred.

"You're still a Chosen, aren't you?" he said, raising his knife. "Do this, do that! We're not your servants down here! We're Freefolk, not Underfolk. And you can wander around down here like little lost light puppets until the guard gets you, as far as I'm concerned!"

Tal raised his Sunstone, his mind concentrating on a Red Ray of Destruction. If Crow sprang at him or tried to throw the knife, he would unleash it.

Crow saw the Red light swirling around the stone and hesitated. Before either of them decided to break the momentary stalemate, Milla sloshed between them and looked up at the Underfolk on the dock.

"There should be no fighting between us, when the real enemy is close," she said. "Afterwards, when the storm is done, we can settle scores."

Crow stared down at her, the fury still obvious in his face. It looked like he was going to attack anyway, until one of the other Underfolk sidled over and whispered something to him.

"Close it, Clovil!" said Crow, pushing the other boy hard enough that he fell over a barrel and into a pile of seaweed.

"All right, I'll say it so everyone can hear," shouted Clovil. He was angry now too, as he clambered out of the seaweed. "We've orders to bring anyone who wants to see Ebbitt to—"

"Close it!" Crow repeated. But he seemed to have lost the heat of his anger, for there was no strength in his words.

"So you *do* know Ebbitt," said Milla. "And there is someone who gives you orders. Lead us to your Crone."

"Our what?" asked Gill, as Crow frowned and did not answer.

"Whoever is in charge," Tal explained. He'd managed to calm himself down and was remembering his first introduction to Milla and the Icecarls. Obviously these Freefolk weren't normal Underfolk and couldn't be treated like them. He'd have to be more polite. He'd learned at least that out on the Ice.

"I'm sorry about what I said," Tal added, looking at Crow. Crow stared at him, expressionless. There was no knowing what thoughts lay behind those unblinking eyes. Tal didn't know whether his apology was accepted or not.

"Clovil, Ferek," Crow ordered, "lead out. We'll go via forge country and across holding tank four."

"Four?" asked Ferek. He was a small and seemingly nervous boy. He twitched as he spoke. Tal had seen that sort of twitch before. Ferek must have spent time in the Hall of Nightmares.

"I said forge country and holding tank four," snapped Crow. "Do I have to repeat every order?"

"Only the stupid ones," muttered Gill, too soft for anyone but Milla to hear. The Icecarl glanced at the girl, who was surprised to have been heard. She scowled and looked away.

Milla and Tal climbed out of the water and on to the dock, their Spiritshadows rising up close behind them. The Underfolk stepped back, unconsciously forming a line.

"As I said, I am Milla of the Far-Raiders Clan of the Icecarls. What are your names?"

The Underfolk all looked at Crow, who shrugged. Evidently this was permission. Even so, it took a moment before they mumbled their names.

"I'm Gill," said the blonde girl. Like all of them, she wore a mixture of Underfolk white robes and odd bits and pieces. In her case, that included the belt from a Blue Brightstar, though the belt was so dirty it could be black instead of blue. She needed it because she was so skinny.

Up close Tal saw that her white Underfolk robes had crude writing on them, as did all the others. He had to crane his head sideways before he could work out that it was the letter F from the standard Chosen alphabet repeated over and over.

"It stands for Freefolk," said Clovil, who had seen

what Tal was doing. "Free of the Chosen. It shows who we are, to separate us from the Fatalists."

"The Fatalists?" asked Tal. "Uh, that starts with F too..."

"But they don't have writing on their robes," Clovil explained.

"You mean the... the regular Underfolk?"

Crow made a cutting movement with his hand and Clovil didn't answer. Tal didn't press it. There was still a lot of tension in the air.

"You are called Clovil?" asked Milla, when no one else introduced themselves.

Clovil nodded. He still had seaweed on his shoulders. He was almost as tall as Crow, and from the way he'd behaved before it looked like he thought he should be in charge. His long sandy hair was held back by a comb made from a large white bone. Possibly a human one, though the Underfolk kept all sorts of livestock for the Chosen's tables so it could easily have come from an animal.

"And you are Ferek," continued Milla, pointing at the twitching small boy. He nodded and smiled eagerly. Crow frowned at him and the smile disappeared.

Apart from Crow that left a single stout girl, who had stood silently by the whole time. Unlike the others, she wore a heavy hide apron over her Underfolk robes and had a large number of pouches hanging from her belt.

"That's Inkie," said Gill.

Inkie nodded to them. There was no explanation of why she didn't talk.

"I am Odris," said Odris, after another momentary pause.

As the Spiritshadow spoke, all the Underfolk – even Crow – jumped in surprise and Ferek stepped back, shaking uncontrollably, as if he had a sudden fever.

"What?" asked Odris, looking at Milla and Tal. "All I said was my name!"

"Spiritshadows don't usually talk to anyone but their masters, in private," said Tal. He'd become so used to Adras and Odris talking away that he'd forgotten this was yet another way in which the Storm Shepherds were different from other Spiritshadows.

"Odris and Adras are not normal Chosen Spiritshadows," explained Tal to the Underfolk. "They are... um... friends, I suppose, rather than... er... servants."

Milla didn't say anything. She was looking back across the lake, into the darkness. Lights had flared there, a sudden show of distant flashes and stars. There was also the very faint echo of shouts.

"The guards," she said urgently. "They've found us. We have to move quickly."

"Right," said Crow. "Like I said – through forge country and then across holding tank four. Clovil, Ferek, you lead."

The two named Underfolk ran along the dock to a door in the cavern wall and slipped through it.

"After you," said Crow to Tal and Milla, gesturing for them to go first.

Milla shook her head.

"No," she said evenly. "We will follow you."

Crow stared for a moment, then shrugged and left, followed by the other Underfolk. On the way, he picked up a long strand of the weed, one with very large nodules, and hung it over his shoulder.

Gill and Inkie did the same.

Milla and Tal waited till the Freefolk were well in front before they followed. Nothing was said, but both Milla and Tal didn't want Crow behind them.

The Freefolk led Milla, Tal and the two Spiritshadows through winding, narrow pathways that were carved roughly through the pale yellow stone of the mountain. Every now and then a single fading Sunstone would show that these ways had once been lit and used by the Chosen. But for the most part they were dark, stained with the smoke from Underfolk lanterns, and the only Sunstones were long dead, nothing more than blackened pits in the ceiling or walls.

Clovil and Ferek kept up a fast pace, which pleased Milla, since she knew the guards or their Spiritshadows would soon work out where they'd gone. It would have pleased Tal too if his leg didn't hurt so much. He wanted to use his Sunstone to ease the pain, but they never stopped long enough for him to cast any of the healing glows he'd learned in the Lectorium.

After an hour of travelling through the narrowest, most winding ways, Clovil and Ferek slowed down and stopped a few stretches before the next corner. As the others moved up, Tal and Milla heard strange water noises – or something – gurgling and splashing, almost as if a herd of giant animals were drinking and then spitting.

There was also a strange light spilling into the tunnel – a hot yellow-and-blue-tinged light that Tal had never seen before. At least, never so intensely. It reminded him of something he couldn't quite place.

"We have to time this bit carefully," said Gill. "Wait for the backflow."

"Backflow of what?" asked Tal.

"The crystal," said Gill. "This is forge country."

"Close it, Gill, and see whose shift is on and how long till the backflow," Crow ordered suddenly.

Gill sniffed and edged up to the corner. As soon as she stuck her head around, her skin was bathed in the yellow-blue light, so she seemed to have changed colour. She looked for a minute and then ducked back.

"It's the Thrower and his gang," Gill reported. "I reckon the backflow's not far away. The crystal's already changing colour."

Her mention of the Thrower's name was met by groans from the other Freefolk, except for Crow. He simply frowned slightly and kept looking at the spill of light around the corner.

"Who is this 'Thrower'?" Milla asked. "Is he an enemy?"

"Not exactly," explained Clovil. "He's a Fatalist, like most of them—"

"Close it!" snapped Crow.

"Close it yourself!" Clovil snapped back. "Like I said, he's a Fatalist, what you call an Underfolk. They think we're all meant to work for the Chosen, that's the way life is meant to be—"

Crow made a threatening move towards Clovil, who immediately closed his mouth with a grimace.

He opened it again once Crow had stepped back.

"We call him the Thrower because he throws liquid crystal at anyone who interferes with the work."

"Liquid crystal?" asked Tal. "What's that?"

"You'll see!" Crow announced. "It's going green. Get ready to run, everyone. Tal and Milla, stay exactly behind us. Don't leave the path."

The light ahead was changing, going from the yellow-blue into a cooler green. When only a few flickers of colour remained and the light was nearly all green, Crow shouted, "Backflow!"

Clovil and Ferek suddenly leapt forward and rounded the corner at a run, the others close behind.

They burst out into a huge cavern. Tal had only a moment to take it all in before he had to concentrate on following the Freefolk.

A narrow, meandering path was appearing in the centre of a huge sea of molten green crystal that was ebbing back towards the sides of the giant cavern. Heat rolled off the crystal in shimmering waves, but it was bearable. Tal couldn't work out why they hadn't all been incinerated immediately, as surely such a lake of molten crystal would have set their clothes alight at least. Then he saw the enormous, ancient Sunstones in the ceiling and the light that they projected.

The Sunstones were melting the crystal liquid at each side of the cavern, but they were also cooling this central path. Other Sunstones were projecting lines of blue force that stirred the crystal, creating eddies and currents.

There were other safe paths appearing as the liquid ebbed, paths that formed around deep pools of crystal. Underfolk clad in heavy protective robes and boots hurried out along the paths to scoop molten crystal from the deeper pools with long-handled ladles. Once their ladle was brimming with liquid crystal, they ran back to one of the three raised islands that were permanently safe from the molten mass. On the island, they poured the liquid crystal into a waiting mould and then ran back out for more.

Tal was busy looking at what the Underfolk were doing and didn't realise he'd fallen behind until he heard Gill scream at him, "Hurry up!"

At the same time, he felt one of the Sunstones above switch off. Without its beneficial blue light the temperature shot up until it was searing. Tal jumped forward and sprinted to catch up with the others, who were just climbing on to the third island. As he landed, his leg spasmed and he half fell, half sat down. He pushed his thumbs into the muscle, grimacing in pain.

"Let me do that," said Adras, reaching his huge, puffy shadow-fingers down. Tal hastily pulled his leg away.

"No! No! You'd probably break my leg."

"This is halfway. We have to wait here for the next backflow," said Gill. "Let's hope the Thrower leaves us alone."

Tal kept massaging his leg and looked out across the cavern. Molten crystal was flowing back across the path and the light was once again growing more intense. It was cool enough on the island, but Tal could tell that this was totally dependent on a single, very old Sunstone. Looking around, he saw charred, corroded lumps of high ground. There had once been more than three islands, but their Sunstones had failed.

"So this is where all the cups and plates are made," Tal said as he watched the Underfolk on the closest island turn the moulds over and tap them to remove the highly durable crystal cups, plates and other utensils he was so familiar with. "I had no idea."

"You wouldn't," said Crow. "The robes and boots those people are wearing are nearly as old as the Sunstones in the ceiling. Do you know how many people burn to death here every year, just so some Chosen can have plates of different colours?"

Behind him, Gill held up her thumb and forefinger to show "zero". Crow must have seen some hint of that in Tal's eyes, because he whirled around angrily. Gill's hand dropped instantly and she looked away. She was clearly afraid of Crow.

"Dark take it," swore Clovil. "It's the Thrower."

He pointed. Through the distorting heat haze above the steadily spreading crystal, now once again mostly a fierce yellow tipped with blue, Tal saw someone wading through the molten mass.

"How's he—" Tal started to say, before he saw

more clearly. The man was wearing the same sort of heavy suit that Tal had seen on the other Underfolk workers, but this one had active Sunstones worked into it. They were wreathing the figure in cool blue light.

"The only armour that still works," said Clovil nervously. "I hope we get the backflow before he gets close enough to throw."

It was slow going through the molten crystal. There were currents and deep holes that had to be waded around. But the Thrower knew them all and he kept on coming. He carried one of the long-handled ladles over his shoulder.

"Maybe he'll only warn us," said Ferek. He was twitching again.

"He warned us last time," said Clovil. "He'll burn us for sure."

"No, he won't," said Crow. "Use your head."

He gestured scornfully at Tal and Milla.

"As soon as he sees these two with their Sunstones and Spiritshadows, he'll be licking their hands and wanting to show them around."

Ferek sighed with relief and relaxed. But Clovil

kept watching the approaching Underfolk. As the Thrower drew closer, he took the ladle off his shoulder and started scooping and throwing big globs of molten crystal in their general direction.

"I don't think the Thrower can see too well," Clovil announced as one of the lumps of crystal splashed down twenty or thirty stretches short of the island. "He's pretty old and he's got a hood and goggles on."

Another superhot glob of crystal hurled through the air, landing even closer.

"I don't think he can see the Spiritshadows or the Sunstones at all," said Clovil, his voice growing more anxious as they all edged to the furthest point of the island. "How long to the backflow?"

"A couple of minutes," said Crow calmly, looking at the colour of the crystal.

Even as he spoke, a lump of molten crystal crashed down on the other end of the island, exploding into sparks and spraying superhot fragments in all directions. Some came within a few stretches of the group. In response they all pressed up against one another on the far end.

"Adras," Tal commanded, "you and Odris go out and tell this Thrower to stop. Stay above the crystal and don't get hit if you can help it. Whatever you do, don't try to catch the crystal or bat it away. Since it's infused with Sunstone light it might be able to hurt you."

"Really?" asked Odris. "We're better off staying here then."

Adras had already started to glide out, but she reached out one billowing shadow-hand and pulled him back by the ear.

"Ow!" exclaimed Adras.

The Thrower paused again to scoop up liquid crystal and then expertly hurled it. This time it splashed down to the left of the huddled group, off the island. They were struck with tiny falling sparks and specks of molten crystal.

Everyone except Milla and Crow jumped and swatted at the burning specks, trying to get them off their clothes before they burned through to the skin.

"Hurry up, Odris," snapped Milla. The Thrower was scooping up crystal again. "You're fast enough to avoid getting hit."

"Oh, all right," grumbled Odris. "I know you just want to get rid of me anyway."

She launched herself up into the air, arms and legs losing definition to become more cloudlike. The cavern was so bright that her shadowflesh was well defined. She looked almost like she had back in Aenir, as a jet-black storm cloud.

Adras followed her, but had to put one foot down on the island and give himself a boost to get into the air. Tal sighed as he saw the clumsy manoeuvre. Disobedient, not too clever and clumsy – that was his Spiritshadow.

The two Spiritshadows floated out towards the Thrower. He had the ladle out of the crystal and was twisting his body to start flinging when he saw the Spiritshadows coming his way.

Surprised, he kept swinging the ladle back until he lost his balance. He dropped the ladle, his arms flailed at the air and then he fell backwards – into the molten crystal. There was a huge splash, a hand clawed above the surface and then he was gone.

There was only the flowing crystal, colour

already changing to blue, and the heat haze shimmering above it.

"He's dead for sure," said Clovil as he stared where only seconds ago there had been a man. "Even with the suit."

The Spiritshadows returned and grew their legs down to walk on the island once more.

"We didn't do anything," said Odris anxiously. "He just fell over."

"He *was* throwing molten crystal at us," said Gill, without much conviction. For a supposedly bloodthirsty rebel, she seemed greatly shocked by this sudden accident.

"Almost backflow," said Crow. He was the only one who seemed unconcerned. "Get ready. We have to get across the rest of the cavern this time."

But everyone was still watching the point where the Thrower had fallen into the crystal. It was cooling now, turning blue-green, and the liquid was ebbing back. No one spoke, but obviously everyone was hoping that the Thrower would have somehow survived, that he would stand up.

The molten crystal continued to flow back to the

sides and the paths started to appear. The Thrower's body became visible, a motionless lump, a tiny island.

"The Sunstones are still working in his suit," said Tal, noting the blue glow. "Maybe we should help him up. He might be all right."

"We haven't got time." Crow pointed to the path that was slowly appearing as the crystal retreated. "It's backflow now!"

He started off to the far side of the cavern. The other Freefolk hesitated, then took off after him. Milla grabbed Tal by the arm and pulled him to follow.

"There's no time," she said. "He was an enemy. The guards are still after us, remember. Come on!"

Tal followed her. He couldn't work out why he felt so upset. The Thrower was only an Underfolk, and Underfolk died all the time. But it was all so sudden. One second he was alive, and then he was drowning in molten crystal...

Perhaps he would still get up, after they'd gone. Perhaps his armour was good enough to keep him alive while he recovered his strength...

Tal's leg started hurting again then and he had to focus his mind on running. It was a good two hundred stretches to the far side of the cavern, and the others were well ahead. Except for Adras, who kept pausing to look back.

Once again, Tal felt the protective rays of the ceiling Sunstones begin to fade. The others were already climbing a steep stair that led out of the cavern. Suddenly the molten crystal began flowing back. Tal was fifty stretches short and he had a moment of panic as a sudden surge of crystal flowed across the path. But it was narrow and he managed to jump it and land without his leg giving way. Even so, he felt the heat, a sudden flash that would have been dangerous if it lasted for more than a split second.

When he gained the steps, Crow looked down at him with a sneer.

"Too much eating and not enough exercising," he said. "Typical Chosen."

"Tal is wounded," explained Milla in a matter-of-fact tone. "A Waspwyrm sting to the leg."

"A what?" asked Clovil.

"Waspwyrm," said Tal. "In the spirit world, Aenir."

"Aenir?" Clovil looked confused. "But I thought the Chosen's bodies stayed behind when they go to Aenir."

"They do," said Tal. "But whatever happens there affects your body here."

"Does it work the other way too?" asked Crow, with a sudden intensity. "If a Chosen's body is hurt here when they're in Aenir, do they hurt there?"

Tal looked at the glitter in Crow's eyes. It was clear that he really hated the Chosen.

"Their bodies are guarded by their Spiritshadows here," Tal said shortly, not really answering the question.

"But what if they weren't protected?" Crow continued. "Say I stabbed a Chosen's body, would he or she die in Aenir?"

"They are guarded by Spiritshadows, so who knows?" replied Tal.

"Maybe I'll find out one day," Crow taunted menacingly.

"Enough talk," commanded Milla. "We can talk later. We need to find Ebbitt."

Crow nodded and jerked his head at Clovil and Ferek, indicating that they should lead off again.

The stair continued up almost to the top of the cavern, where it ended in a set of very large metal doors. They were slightly ajar, just enough for people to slip between, though someone as fat as Sushin would have trouble.

Milla paused at the doors, brushing the dust from a small patch. As she'd thought, the doors were made of the same dull golden metal as the Icecarls' Ruin Ship, and Asteyr's Orskir, in the spirit world. Further evidence of the connection between the Icecarls and the Chosen, way back in distant times.

Tal paused too, but it was to look down at the forge country's molten sea. Even this high up, he could feel the heat coming off the crystal, and the counterbalancing cool of the Sunstones set in the ceiling, which was still higher than the top of the stair.

He scanned the area near the central island, hoping to see some sign of the Thrower. But there was no one there. There were only Underfolk on the other islands, busy at their work.

It was possible that the Thrower had got up and made it back to one of those other islands as they climbed the stairs. But it was unlikely.

"Tal."

It was Milla calling. She waved her hand, telling him to hurry.

Tal kept looking. Adras was next to him, looking down as well.

"Pretty colours," said Adras. "Like rainbows."

Tal couldn't see anything pretty in the molten crystal. Just the memory of a human hand clawing for support, desperate for help, the last action of a dying man as he sank beneath the burning surface.

"Tal!"

"I've never seen anyone die," whispered Tal. "Not like that. So suddenly."

Milla came back, frowning. But it was not a frown of anger.

"Death is the end of a song," she explained quietly. "But it is not the end of all songs. Here, a man has died. Somewhere, in your castle or out upon the ice, a child has been born. One song ends, another begins."

Tal looked at Milla. She had surprised him again.

"Did you just make that up?"

"No," replied Milla. "I learned it, long ago. Hurry up!"

The Freefolk led them through another maze of narrow passages, all of them dark. Some were partially flooded, requiring wading. Others were packed with long-forgotten boxes and barrels, rotting away in the darkness. Occasionally bright patches of luminous mould shone like pale beacons, and once a Sunstone flickered high on a wall, a stone in its dying days.

They saw no other Underfolk and it was clear that the paths Crow chose were rarely used by anyone. More than once, Clovil and Ferek hesitated before a choice of ways, and there was a quick conference with Crow before they moved off again.

After several hours, they climbed down a switchbacked series of rough-hewn steps, to enter a large cavern with a sandy floor. Crow led them to the centre and declared they would take a rest.

"We don't need a rest," said Milla. "We need to meet with Ebbitt. Then I have to go on."

Tal didn't say anything. He needed a rest. His leg was aching and he wanted to take the pain away with some healing light. He gratefully sat down on one of the stones Crow had indicated in the centre of the cavern and stretched out his leg.

The others kept standing, a few stretches away. Adras slid over and copied Tal, stretching out his puffy leg.

"My leg hurts too," he announced.

Odris came over to look at it, while Tal focused on his Sunstone to summon a Blue Glow of Healing. It wasn't as powerful as the full Blue Ray, but at least it would take the pain away.

Concentrating on the light magic, Tal didn't really pay attention to what the others were doing. Milla was arguing with Crow about the delay, and the other Freefolk had drifted over to stand behind him, except for Inkie, who had wandered over to the far side of the cavern and appeared to be looking at the rock wall.

Tal was unprepared when, in midsentence, Crow leapt forward and pushed Milla as hard as he could. She flew back, turning into a flip as she fell. She landed on her feet, knife suddenly in her hand.

Before she could do anything, Crow shouted, "Now!"

Even before he shouted, Inkie pulled a concealed lever in the wall.

The floor below Tal suddenly opened, sand cascading down. Tal yelled and tried to jump up and across, but it was too late.

The whole centre of the cavern was a trapdoor. Tal went down with the cascading sand, Adras following him with an excited shout.

Milla was quicker. As the floor shifted, she threw herself forward and got a handhold on the lip of the huge trapdoor – but she had to drop her knife. Odris flew up behind her and gripped her around the waist, easily lifting her on to solid ground.

Crow charged her immediately, with Clovil and

Gill coming on each side. Ferek ran around the outside, yelling excitedly.

Milla met Crow's charge with a flurry of punches and kicks. Crow surprised her by blocking or dodging most of them, until she got a lock on his arm and used it to swing him around to collect a blow from Clovil.

Milla had to let Crow go then, as Gill tried to grab her around the knees and push her over into the hole. Milla jumped clear and followed up with a kick that knocked Gill out.

"Odris!" she shouted. "Attack!"

"But Adras has gone down there," said Odris, pointing at the hole. She didn't attack.

Milla scowled in anger. Crow and Clovil circled her warily. Ferek had retreated to join Inkie. Gill was groaning on the ground.

"Why?" asked Milla. "We had an agreement."

"Can't trust a Chosen," said Crow. He drew a long, sharp knife. Clovil looked at him, then hesitantly drew his own knife.

"What about Ebbitt?" said Milla. She didn't take her eyes off either knife-wielding opponent.

"And your Crone? Your leader?"

"What they don't know won't bother them," Crow replied.

Clovil glanced across at his leader. Milla saw the uncertainty there.

"Someone will tell them," she said. Crow smiled and edged forward, his knife weaving slightly from side to side.

"I could let you go," he said, "if you promise to just get out of here. We'll take you to the heatways. You aren't a Chosen. I've got the one I wanted. That Tal. Once a Chosen, always a Chosen."

"We have to help Adras," said Odris. "He hasn't come back up."

Milla thought about it for a moment. She could feel Odris's desire to fly down to see what had happened to Adras.

Inkie moved. For a fraction of a second, Milla was distracted.

In that moment, Crow reversed his knife, revealing a Sunstone in its pommel. The stone flashed white. Milla and Odris cried out and shielded their eyes.

At the same moment, even more of the floor opened up. Milla fell back, flailing her arms and legs. Accompanied by a torrent of sand, she slid down into darkness, Odris fleeing after her.

Behind them, Milla heard a panicked shout and saw someone else tumble into the sandslide above her.

It was Gill. She had been caught too, and she, Milla and Odris were all plummeting down.

There was no way to break their fall, though Milla did manage to turn herself around so she was sliding feet first. And she called up light from her Sunstone.

As she spun and slid along with a large quantity of sand, she saw they were on some sort of steep ramp. A very long, steep ramp. Already she'd lost sight of the trapdoor above them, though it had probably closed again.

Gill was twenty or thirty stretches behind her, upside down and screaming as she tumbled.

Odris was ahead, on her back, her arms and legs spread out wide. She appeared to be enjoying the ride.

"Odris! Slow me down!" Milla shouted.

For once, the Spiritshadow obeyed. She made herself puffier and flew back against the sliding sand. Milla put her feet on the Spiritshadow's shoulders and felt herself slow. A few seconds later, she caught Gill as the Freefolk girl slid past.

An immediate headlock indicated that Milla hadn't grabbed the other girl out of kindness.

"Where does this go?" Milla demanded. The rushing sand was very noisy, as well as uncomfortable. They would be minus some skin by the time they got to the bottom.

Gill coughed and spluttered, unable to answer. She'd got a lot of sand in her face. Milla contented herself by keeping hold of the girl. Questions – and answers – could wait till they got to the bottom.

They didn't have long to wait. The ramp suddenly grew steeper and Odris groaned at the extra effort of slowing them down. Then suddenly they shot out into open air, high up in some vast cavern.

"Odris!" Milla shouted again as she fell off the Spiritshadow's shoulders and lost her grip on Gill. She was falling and the ground was a hundred stretches below. Milla concentrated on keeping her eyes open. Icecarls always faced death with their eyes open.

Odris grabbed her a second later. She had Gill in her other hand, but the combined weight of both girls was too much for the Spiritshadow to fly. They continued to fall, too fast for comfort.

A few seconds later, they hit.

Not solid stone or sand, but warm water. All three went under with a huge splash, and all three came back up again.

Milla spat out a mouthful of water and swam a few strokes in a circle, looking around. She could see Gill coughing and spluttering, but she was all right. Odris was puffing herself up, climbing out of the water into the air.

There was no sign of Tal at first. Then Milla saw a bright Sunstone light, fifty or sixty stretches away and higher up.

"Over here!" shouted Tal. "Hurry!"

Milla spat out even more water and started to swim. Her furs were heavy and already waterlogged, but she had learned to swim that way, in the warm pools around the Smoking Mountain.

"Hurry!" Tal yelled again. He sounded scared. Milla looked around, wondering why. Gill was already swimming as fast as she could towards Tal. Odris was floating above Milla, unconcerned.

What could Tal see that she couldn't? And what did Gill know about this place that was making her swim so fast?

"Spiders!" Tal shouted. "Hurry!"

Milla focused on her Sunstone, making it brighter, and swung her hand behind her, sending the beam of light flashing across the water. It was met by many sparkling reflections, clusters of bright eyes.

Water spiders. Lots and lots of water spiders.

Milla twisted in the water and started swimming as fast as she could. There were too many reflecting eyes behind her. The whole place was thick with water spiders. She remembered Ebbitt talking about them. They were about half her size, their bulbous bodies were thick-skinned and hard to damage, and they could walk on the water as well as swim in it.

They were also very poisonous.

Milla turned to take a breath and saw a ray of Red light shoot over her head and strike somewhere behind her. She heard the hiss of steaming water and a weird clacking noise, like the grinding of bone planks in an iceship as it ran over rough ground. It took her a moment to realise that it had to be the noise of the spiders' multijointed limbs.

They were racing after her, legs skimming the surface. Tal was trying to keep them at bay with his Sunstone. She saw more Red Rays zap overhead and more steam spouted up behind her. But the clicking was louder too and she redoubled her efforts, kicking harder and pushing all the strength of her shoulders and arms into her stroke.

Somewhere along the way she overtook Gill, who was struggling, her arms and legs flailing, all rhythm lost.

Milla slowed momentarily and looked back. Red Rays of Destruction from Tal's Sunstone criss-crossed the water, sending up gusts of steam. She could feel the heat of them passing overhead. In their light, she could see hundreds of water spiders. A solid line of them, skittering and dancing on the surface. Constantly edging forward, hesitating as Tal's rays struck them, then coming forward again.

"Odris!" called Milla. She couldn't see the Spiritshadow, but she shouted anyway. "Help Gill!"

Something erupted from the water near here, and Milla almost struck at it before she realised it was Odris.

"Too dangerous up there," said the Spiritshadow, indicating the Red Rays flickering off and on above their heads. She reached out and grabbed Gill, who shrieked and went under for a moment, then re-emerged, coughing, as Odris lifted her partially out of the water.

Milla grabbed Odris too. The Spiritshadow had formed her back half into one energetic tail, which was propelling her far faster than Milla could swim.

That was only a fraction faster than the water spiders. They reached the ledge where Tal was kneeling in deep concentration, his Sunstone ring bright Red, rays bursting from it every few seconds. Adras leaned down and pulled Gill out, and Milla leapt up, using Odris's shoulder as a step.

"Too many!" Tal gasped. He waved his hand across the whole front of the ledge, creating a continuous Red Ray that touched the water so that a curtain of steam rose all around the ledge. Water spiders clacked and there was a multitude of splashes as they fell back.

For a moment or two more kept crawling up, even as Tal shot them down.

The ledge was narrow, a crumbling shelf in the cavern's side. It went back only five or six stretches. There was a corridor beyond it, through the cavern side, but the way was barred by a portcullis of golden metal – a heavy grille of cross-hatched bars, set too close together to crawl through.

"Odris! Adras! Help me open this!" Milla shouted. She strained at the portcullis, trying to lift it. But it didn't budge.

The two Spiritshadows flowed across to join her. But when their hands met the golden metal, their shadowflesh went straight through. They couldn't get a grip on it.

"Aarrggghh!"

It was Tal screaming.

Milla spun around to see a huge bloated spider leap on top of Tal. He fell back and its eight hairy legs wrapped completely around him. A second later it struck at his chest with its two huge fangs, venom dripping as it pulled away.

Milla rushed at the spider and kicked it in its disgustingly swollen abdomen, until its legs uncurled and Tal rolled out. Then she spun on her heel and kicked it again, knocking it back into two other water spiders.

"Adras! Odris! Help!"

Without Tal's Red Rays of Destruction to keep them back, the water spiders swarmed the ledge. Milla stood over Tal's body, kicking and punching, and the Spiritshadows stood at her shoulders, their massive arms whirling to knock the spiders back into the water.

Gill hung on to the portcullis, screaming for help.

But no help came. Only more spiders.

With the help of the two Spiritshadows, Milla managed to beat back the spiders' assault and drag Tal to the portcullis, to gain some slight shelter at their backs. But as the water spiders withdrew, it was clear it was only a temporary respite. They were climbing up the wall, spinning sticky threads of web behind them.

"They're getting ready to drop down on us," said Milla, watching the spiders climb. "They'll attack from above as well as in front. Gill! How do you open this portcullis?"

"From outside," sobbed the girl. "Crow will come and get us."

Milla scowled and looked back at the massed ranks of spiders. All those glistening eyes, reflecting in the light of her Sunstone. If only she knew how to create the Red Ray of Destruction, or some of the other light magic Tal had told her about. Even better would be her Merwin-horn sword or an Icecarl battle-axe. Then the water spiders would keep their distance.

But she had only her fists and feet. Even her knife was lost.

A sudden thought came to her. The other Freefolk had knives. Perhaps Gill did too.

"Gill, give me your knife," she ordered. The Freefolk girl was still screaming through the bars of the portcullis, so Milla had to shout at her twice. Numbly, the girl pulled a long, thin knife from the side of her boot and handed it to Milla.

Milla smiled as she brandished it. The knife was metal and sharp, and it glistened in the light more brightly than the spiders' eyes.

She would make the spiders pay dearly for her life. She hadn't managed to kill any spiders with her blows, but she would now.

"Ten," she whispered. That seemed a reasonable number of spiders to take as a death-due for her own life. "And five for Tal."

The water spiders were almost directly above Milla. A thin wisp of spider-silk fell down across her shoulders. The front rank of spiders began to click and rustle as they moved forward in a single line. Their horrible hairy legs rose and fell in near-perfect synchronisation as they edged forward, their fangs twitching and dripping with venom.

Their eyes, thought Milla. She would have to stab them in the eyes.

"Adras, Odris. I want you to hold each one in front of me, so I can stick them. Then throw it back and grab the next one."

"I feel sleepy," said Adras, yawning. "Very sleepy."

"Not now!" exclaimed Milla. But even as she spoke, the huge Spiritshadow slipped down the wall and spread out on the ground, across the still form of Tal.

"Adras!" exclaimed Odris, and she slid down too, to see what was wrong with him.

The spiders chose that moment to attack. Dozens

of them rushed forward, running on one another's backs and getting tangled in their eagerness to get at their prey. Others dropped straight down, or swung in on webs.

Milla shouted her war cry, Gill screamed something – and suddenly the water spiders stopped and reeled back. Milla stared at them as they fell over each other trying to get away.

Surely her war cry wasn't that effective?

A moment later a great cloud of foul-smelling mist rolled past her. It was a foul smell she recognised, though she had last experienced it as a yellow ointment.

Ebbitt's water spider repellent.

She turned around. The portcullis was up, and there was Ebbitt and his maned Spiritshadow. The old man had a small barrel under his arm and a pumping device. He was working vigorously to spray repellent everywhere.

Gill was dragging Tal through the gate and Odris was dragging Adras.

"Hurry up, hurry up, don't be late for the gate," said Ebbitt. Milla hurried through. Ebbitt backed after her, still spraying. When he was through, the portcullis rumbled down.

"A spider bit Tal," said Milla. "I couldn't stop it."

"Well now, I don't suppose you could." Ebbitt didn't appear to be terribly concerned. "They're awful biters when the mood strikes them. Which is most of the time. You and young Gillimof will have to carry him."

"I told you not to call me that," Gill protested.

Milla was about to ask Ebbitt how he knew where they were. Then she saw Crow and the other Freefolk standing by a large wheel that obviously raised and lowered the portcullis. Instantly she pushed past Ebbitt, knife held low for a savage cut.

"Traitor!"

Before she could reach him, Ebbitt's Spiritshadow reared up between them and a sparkling loop of Indigo light wrapped around Milla's torso and pulled her back.

"Let me go!" roared Milla. "He promised to bring us to you and then dropped us in with the water spiders!"

"That's what we're supposed to do for

suspicious visitors," said Crow easily. "And *all* Chosen. So we can leave them in with the water spiders if we need to."

"That's true," said Ebbitt. "A precaution insisted upon by the leader of the Freefolk. Only the blue-tufted flowershrike here was a little slow letting me know."

"Crow!" corrected Crow, touching the black feathers in his hat. "You know I'm called Crow!"

"What about Tal?" asked Milla. "I told you a spider bit him."

"And something's happened to Adras as well!" added Odris. "I can't wake him up!"

Ebbitt peered at Odris, who had her fellow Spiritshadow draped over her shoulders. He looked at them through both eyes, then only through his left eye, shutting the right. He tried looking with his left eye shut and right eye open, then with both shut.

Finally he opened both eyes again and said, "Storm Shepherds, I believe? And in free association, not bound?"

"Yes," said Odris.

"Well, won't lots of Chosen be running around gibbering when they hear about you!" Ebbitt exclaimed. "Now, don't worry about Tal and... um... Pladros. The spider venom is only a soporific in small doses and the Fleefolk have an antidote."

"That's Freefolk, not Fleefolk!" corrected Crow.

"What is a soporific?" asked Milla. The word was unfamiliar to her, though much of the Chosen and Icecarl language was the same.

"Something that puts you to sleep," explained Ebbitt. "It can be a drug or something else, as in the sentence 'Blueshrike's tales of his bravery were extremely soporific'."

Gill and Clovil laughed, but choked it back as Crow glared at them.

"Come on then," said Ebbitt, clapping his hands. "Milla and Gill, you can carry Tal. We must be off to the Leefolk's lair. I mean the Weefolk's weir. That is, the Freefolk's fortress. Where is the Codex, by the way? Under your coat perhaps? We'll need it for the meeting."

"It's up in the Mausoleum," replied Milla. "We had to hide it there. It was too big to carry."

Ebbitt stopped and a look of genuine consternation spread across his face.

"You mean you left it behind? It's the one thing we really need! You should have left yourselves behind!"

"We brought it back from Aenir and that wasn't easy," retorted Milla. "But we hid it. It will still be in the Mausoleum."

"No, no, no it won't!" Ebbitt howled. He started jumping up and down on the spot. "It can move of its own accord in the Castle at least, if not further afield. It will wander off! It could be anywhere!"

"It was too big to carry," said Milla angrily. "We were lucky to get away ourselves. Besides, it is nothing to me. I am returning to my people."

"It shrinks," said Ebbitt mournfully. "You could have carried it. Or asked it to follow you."

"I don't care," said Milla. "I will help carry Tal to your Freefolk Fortress and then I am leaving. I am going back to the Ice."

The Freefolk Fortress, as Ebbitt called it, lay on the far side of a deep chasm that went all the way down to the lava pools that the Chosen had tapped long ago for their complex heating systems of steam and hot water. As they approached the lip of the chasm, Milla could feel the heat rising up from the depths and could see the red glow.

The only way across was a narrow, makeshift bridge that precariously spanned the fifty-stretch gap. The basic structure of the bridge was two very narrow rails of the same golden metal as the Ruin Ship. But all the planking and the handrailings were made of crystal, metal and scavenged material of all kinds that could easily be dismantled so that the bridge would be almost impossible to cross.

Fortunately, it seemed solid enough as they crossed it, though Milla was careful to watch where she stepped and not put any undue reliance on the handrails. She and Gill were carrying Tal between them, so it was slow progress. Odris was carrying Adras and complaining about it every ten or twelve steps.

Ebbitt led the way in his own peculiar fashion, stopping every now and then to spin round, or suddenly crouch down, or just stop and stare into space. His maned Spiritshadow watched him indulgently, itself always regal and controlled.

Across the chasm they passed through a narrow, winding tunnel. Milla noted holes in the ceiling, useful for throwing stones or pouring hot liquid on intruders. With the chasm and this narrow way, the Freefolk were well defended. Though Milla doubted any of it would be much use against determined Chosen, with their Spiritshadows and Sunstone magic.

Since Tal had never mentioned the Freefolk, she

suspected that the Chosen either didn't know about the Underfolk rebels or simply didn't care about them, as long as they didn't cause too much trouble.

The narrow tunnel finally opened out into a vast cavern, easily three or four hundred stretches in diameter and more than a hundred stretches deep. A few old, pinkish Sunstones shone in the distant ceiling, creating an effect like an Aeniran twilight.

There were six or seven fairly dumpy cottages arranged in a circle in the middle of the cavern, centred on a large open well, with clear water lapping over its sides into a gutter. A few buckets were stacked next to the well, and there was a pile of barrels, boxes and other containers in a walled pen behind the houses.

It didn't look like much. It certainly didn't look like a fortress.

"The Fortress of the Freefolk," announced Ebbitt, with a grand gesture. "Or Temporary Digging Camp Fourteen as it was once known many, many, many caveroach lives ago."

"Where do we take Tal?" Milla asked. The Chosen

boy was heavy and, though she would never admit it, Milla was tired.

"Oh, I suppose I can give him the antidote here as well as anywhere," said Ebbitt. He took a small vial out of one of the deep pockets of his multilayered robe and added, "Just lay him down and support his head."

"You have the antidote on you?" asked Milla. "You had it all the time? Why didn't you use it before?"

"The poor boy clearly needed his rest," said Ebbitt, looking down on his great-nephew.

Milla shook her head. She knew there was no point in getting angry with Ebbitt. He was like some of the older Crones. His mind was travelling somewhere else where no ordinary Icecarl – or Chosen – could follow.

She and Gill laid Tal down and then held up his head. Ebbitt bent down and opened the sleeping boy's mouth with two fingers, poured in the contents of the vial, pinched Tal's nose and said, "Shake him up and down a bit."

Milla and Gill followed his instructions. Nothing happened at first, then Tal coughed. The cough was followed by a sneeze, suffocated by Ebbitt's nose-clasping fingers. Then Tal's eyes slowly opened. He was groggy, but after a minute or so he could stand up on his own.

At the same time, Adras came round and sat up, scratching his head.

"Why did you wake me up?" he said aggrievedly to Odris. "I was having such a good dream. I was shooting lightning at moths and every time I hit one they exploded with smoke and sparks—"

Odris slapped him, shadowflesh meeting shadowflesh with a strange rasping sound.

"I thought you were dying!" she said. "And you're worried about a stupid dream!"

"Where are we?" asked Tal. His voice was weak and he felt terrible. He was sick in the stomach and shivery all over.

"The Freefolk Fortress," said Ebbitt.

"The Cavern of the Freefolk," said Crow at the same time. "Call it by its proper name."

He pushed past Ebbitt and stalked off towards the largest of the cottages. Inkie scuttled after him. Clovil and Ferek hesitated then followed. Gill stayed behind.

As Crow approached the cottage, the door opened and two grown men in the painted Underfolk robes came out. One was quite old, as old as Ebbitt, but he was much shorter and quite shrivelled and dried-up-looking. He had grey hair, cut so short it was a stubble. The other man was about the same age as Tal's father, Rerem, though he was much brawnier. He looked like the sort of Underfolk who did the heavy carrying around the Castle. His chest and upper body were easily twice the size of Tal's. His hair was black and long.

As Tal looked at the younger man, he realised he had to be related to Crow and might even be his father. There was a strong facial resemblance and though Crow was not physically as big yet, there was every indication he would be one day.

Crow raised his hand in a formal-looking salute, but only the older man waved back. Tal was surprised to see Crow lean forward and hug his brawny relative, but the man did not hug him in return.

"We have brought four prisoners," Crow said to the older man, loud enough for Tal and Milla to hear easily. "Two Chosen and two Spiritshadows."

"I'm not a Chosen," Milla declared. "And I'm not a prisoner."

Tal didn't say anything. He didn't feel up to it. Besides, after his experience with the Icecarls he had started to think that silence was the best policy when meeting anyone new.

"Neither am I," said Odris. "And Adras isn't one either."

"One what?" asked Adras. He was rubbing his stomach and hadn't been listening.

"Prisoner. You're not a prisoner of anybody!" said Odris.

"Sure." Adras looked across at Tal and said, "Can you try to feel better? Your shadow is making me feel sick. It made me sleepy before."

"It's the spider bite," Tal explained. "So you were unconscious too?"

"And asleep," Adras answered. "I fell over right after you did."

Crow and the other Freefolk were talking to the old men, but Tal didn't listen. He was too interested in what Adras had just said.

"I wonder if this spider poison..." he said aloud. Then he turned to Ebbitt and said, "Uncle Ebbitt? Could my mother be ill because she's being poisoned with water spider venom?"

Ebbitt scratched his head, and discovered a blue crayon that had somehow got tangled there. He looked at it in a puzzled way and said, "Yes. I hadn't thought of that! I don't know how you would get the venom out of the spider. But constant small doses would make her very sleepy and, if continued, would force a coma. Yes, it explains the symptoms. But how to milk the spider? I suppose some sort of harness and then a vacuum apparatus. Good thick gloves, a stick to whack the critter with..."

His voice trailed off into a mumble as he continued to think aloud.

"Gref must have been poisoned too," said Tal. He was thinking furiously as he became more alert. Both his mother and Gref poisoned with water spider venom... Sushin must have access to the spiders. Perhaps he even had some tame ones somewhere...

Tal shuddered at the thought of Sushin cuddling

up with water spiders. But he was also suddenly hopeful. Now that he suspected what was being done to Graile and Gref, he could possibly get them the antidote.

His thinking was interrupted by Crow shouting something and stalking off to one of the other cottages. He opened the door viciously, went through and slammed it shut so hard that some rock dust fell from the distant ceiling of the cavern.

The two men watched him go for a moment. Then the older man walked up to Tal, with the black-haired giant following him a pace behind. As they approached, Tal realised the leader looked familiar, though he had never seen him in the robes of an Underfolk... that is... a Freefolk.

"Greetings, Tal and Milla, Odris and Adras," the man said. As Tal heard his deep, measured, vibrant voice, so out of place coming from the little body, he remembered where he'd seen him before.

"I am called Jarnil and I am the leader of the Freefolk," said the old man.

Tal blinked. He knew this man by his full name. He was the Brilliance Jarnil Yannow-Kyr of the

Indigo Order, once Chief Lector. He had taught Tal when he was a little boy.

He had also been dead for at least five years.

10

Tal still remembered the announcement at the Lectorium of the Chief Lector's demise. An accidental death, they'd said, without giving any details. Since any sort of fatal accident was unusual for a Chosen, the children had talked about it for some time, trying to imagine exactly what had happened.

"You're supposed to be dead," Tal burst out.

Jarnil smiled, but it was a bitter smile that did not light up his eyes.

"That was the story they spread," he said. "It was almost true."

He raised his arm and Tal saw that his hand

twitched and jerked as if it had a life of its own, beyond Jarnil's control.

"I was taken to a place you... you know of," said Jarnil. "After Fashnek had finished with me, my supposedly dead body was thrown out to be removed by the Underfolk. That was Fashnek's mistake, for I was dying, not dead.

"For many years I have secretly coordinated the activities of those Underfolk and Chosen who wish to change the way we all live in the Castle. Some of the Underfolk who knew me were on the burial detail. They brought me here and nursed me back to... well, I suppose you could call it health."

"What do you mean Underfolk and Chosen who want to change the way we live?" asked Tal. He was shocked by the idea. He didn't want to change anything. He just wanted everything to go back to normal, with his father and mother at home, with Gref and Kusi. Obviously things would have to change with the Underfolk – and the Icecarls – but perhaps it could be a slow change. Though even as Tal thought that he knew it was too late.

Everything was going to change and he might as well get used to it.

"Exactly that," said Jarnil. "This is Bennem, by the way."

Bennem gave a kind of grunt and nodded a fraction. He seemed about as friendly as Crow. Now that he was closer, Tal thought he wasn't old enough to be Crow's father. Perhaps he was an older brother.

Jarnil kept on talking as he led them to the nearest cottage. Surprisingly, inside the door there were steps leading down to a comfortable, Sunstone-lit cellar room that was much larger than the cottage above it. A thick red rug in the centre of the room was surrounded by low cushions of white and gold. Jarnil sat down and gestured to everyone to sit as well. They all did so, except for Ebbitt, who prowled around the outside, and the Spiritshadows, who floated up to the ceiling to circle the Sunstone set there.

"Where was I?" continued Jarnil. "There is sweetwater in the jugs over there. Help yourselves. Ah, yes. There have always been some Chosen who believe that the Underfolk are no different than we are, save for the accident of their birth. Why should they be kept in ignorance of Sunstone magic, and of Aenir? We called ourselves the Sharers of Light. Similarly, there have always been some Underfolk who have questioned why they should be servants of the Chosen. Though there is some, ah, variation in their aims, they generally call themselves the Freefolk. Together, we hope to change things so that it is possible for capable Underfolk to rise up to Red and become Chosen."

"But you will still have your thralls," said Milla. Her tone of voice showed that she didn't think much of the Sharers of Light.

"Thralls?" asked Jarnil.

"Slaves," replied Milla.

"No, no," said Jarnil. "You don't understand. We cannot change everything. Change must be introduced slowly. We are still loyal to the Empress. All we want to do is test and train Underfolk, and those who show potential to become Chosen will be raised up. Then they may begin their climb to Violet."

Tal shook his head. This all sounded like a Lector's theory, not something practical. Even after only a few moments of thought he knew it wouldn't work.

"Why were you taken to the Hall of Nightmares?" he asked.

Jarnil coughed and a faint hint of redness touched his cheeks.

"I made... er... two serious errors of judgement," he said quickly. "Progress was slow in recruiting Chosen to the Sharers of Light and I had made contact with only a few isolated bands of Freefolk in the lower depths. So I decided to put my plan for raising up Freefolk to the Empress. My first mistake was to share the exact nature of my plan with the Dark Vizier who recorded my request for an audience with Her Majesty. I was granted an audience for the following day. But that night, I was taken..."

His hands shook even more and he had difficulty getting out the last words.

"...To the Hall of Nightmares."

"The Dark Vizier?" asked Tal. He'd never heard of that office. "Who is that?"

"What are they teaching in the Lectorium these days? The Empress has always been served by both a Light Vizier and a Dark Vizier, one for the day and one for the night. Traditionally the Light Vizier deals with ceremony and celebration, while the Dark Vizier deals with matters less pleasant, those best left unseen in darkness. The identity of the Dark Vizier is always kept secret and he or she is disguised as a Chosen of lesser rank, while secretly holding the highest rank in the Violet Order. As is traditional, I met the Dark Vizier in a room where I stood in brilliant light and he in darkness. It was there I made my second mistake..."

"What was that?" asked Tal as Jarnil stopped speaking and stared into the distance.

"I looked back at the doorway as I left," said Jarnil. "The Dark Vizier was careless. He had stepped half out of the shadow, so that the light fell upon his face. I recognised him and I was fool enough to show it."

"Who was it?" asked Tal.

"I think you know," said Jarnil. "Someone who

can speak with the authority of the Empress, command her guards, make other Chosen do his will, all without Her Majesty's knowledge?"

"Sushin!" Tal exclaimed. "But why? What does he hope to gain?"

"Good question," interrupted Ebbitt. "Very good question. When you find out the answer, let me know."

"We do not know what drives Sushin," said Jarnil. "Or to what end. But he has clearly been working towards some evil purpose for many years. I thought I knew him once, but even before my 'disappearance' he had become strange and distant. A different man from the one I used to know."

"He is not a man," said Milla, stirred by the image of Sushin laughing with the Merwin-horn sword thrust through his chest. "I think a Spiritshadow lives inside his flesh. An old shadow that has not forgot the ancient war between our world and Aenir. A shadow that wants to lower the Veil and remove the darkness that protects us. I am sure of this and I will tell the Crones, so that we

Icecarls can do what must be done. I must go back to the Ice."

11

Silence greeted Milla's words, but it was the silence of disbelief rather than shock. Jarnil even smiled a little, the same smile Tal had seen when a Chosen gave a particularly stupid answer in the Lectorium.

Tal opened his mouth to say something, but no words came out. Half of him wanted to protest, to say that Milla was mad, that she had no idea what she was talking about. But the other half wanted to scream out, "Listen to her!"

What she had said *did* make sense. Maybe Zicka the lizard in Aenir had been telling the truth about an ancient war between the Aenirans and the peoples of the Dark World – Chosen and Icecarls.

Something was being done to the Veil, something that Tal's own father had been caught up in, as Guardian of the Orange Keystone. But what was a Guardian? What did the Keystones do?

Tal was about to ask a question about Keystones when he finally noticed something else.

Jarnil had a natural shadow. His Spiritshadow was gone.

"Your Spiritshadow!" gasped Tal, his question forgotten. "What happened to it?"

Jarnil looked down, his natural shadow mimicking the movement exactly, better than any Spiritshadow ever could. No Spiritshadow was that flexible, unlike the shadowguards of children.

"I don't know," he said, the pain of his loss clear on his face. "I believe it was somehow forced to return my natural shadow, which bound it to me, and was then killed, or returned to Aenir, or—"

"Or signed on to serve the good ship Sushin," interrupted Ebbitt gloomily. "Or Fashnek."

"What?" asked Tal. "You mean they took your Spiritshadow and made it serve Sushin?"

"I fear so," said Jarnil. "Fashnek certainly had

more than his own Spiritshadow to do his bidding."

"He has three by my count," said Milla. "As well as the one that carries him. You Chosen have let these shadows in, and they will destroy the Veil and let in the sun. I must go swiftly to tell the Crones. Who will guide me to the heatway tunnels?"

"All in good time, all in good time," soothed Jarnil. "Let us share our knowledge first. What is this talk of the Veil being destroyed?"

"Drunkards talk while warriors work," spat Milla. She got to her feet and glared at the Freefolk. "I know what must be done."

"Yes, yes," said Jarnil. "Gill will take you in due course. Do we have plenty of airweed?"

The last question was directed at the Freefolk girl. She nodded and showed the strand that was tucked through her belt.

"The others have more too," she said. "And there are six barrels to pick up later."

"Airweed?" asked Milla. "What for?"

"Like it says. Airweed for air," said Gill. She indicated one of the bloated nodules. "These hold air. You can tap them with a knife and breathe from them when there is poison air or smoke in the tunnels. That's how we rescued you before."

"Good," said Milla. "Then we will go."

"No!" Tal shouted out. "Wait! Maybe you're right about the Aenirans, and the ancient war and everything, but shouldn't we at least see if Ebbitt, Jarnil and Bennem know anything the Crones need to know?"

Bennem grunted as his name was mentioned again. Tal looked at him in surprise. The surprise turned to pity as he realised that Bennem's eyes were empty, that they were not focused on anything.

Ebbitt noticed him looking.

"He was carried to the Hall with a cry and a shout," Ebbitt explained. "Twice he went in and twice came out. But what went in was more than this, and what didn't come out we'll sorely miss."

"He means that my brother was taken to the Hall of Nightmares twice. His body came back but inside he is dreaming. He knows his name and simple things. Sometimes he wakes fully, but only for a minute or two."

It was Crow speaking. He stood halfway down the steps, with the others behind him. Tal had not heard them come in.

"Our parents did not come out of the Hall," he added, looking straight at Tal. "So you see we have much to thank the Chosen for."

Tal couldn't meet his gaze. He couldn't look at Bennem either. A strange feeling gripped him, a coldness in his stomach. It was guilt, he knew.

"Tal is no longer a Chosen," said Milla. "He is an Outcast. You cannot blame him for the evil of his former clan."

Tal looked at her. Why was she standing up for him?

Crow ignored Milla and turned to Gill, who stepped back a little.

"Come on, Gill. We've got to go back for the barrels."

Gill shook her head. "I'm showing Milla how to get to the heatways."

Crow scowled. "We need you to help with the airweed. She has a Spiritshadow. Let *it* find the way for her. Let her get lost, if it comes to that."

"I'm not an *it*," growled Odris. She billowed down, and Milla slipped into a fighting crouch. Suddenly conflict seemed seconds away.

"No, no!" said Jarnil. "This is all going wrong! Crow, we need to talk to these people, not fight them! Why don't you get Korvim to help with the weed?"

"Korvim and his lot have gone back," Crow replied. "To rejoin the Fatalists. Just like Linel and Drenn and all the others, because we sit around talking all the time instead of killing Chosen!"

"How many Freefolk are there?" asked Tal.

All the Freefolk began to speak at the same time.

"Well, the numbers fluctuate—" began Jarnil.

"Don't tell the spy—" spat Crow.

"Seven right now," said Ferek. "Counting Jarnil."

"Close it!" roared Crow. Ferek flinched, but the older boy did not follow through with any action to enforce his words.

"Close it," repeated Crow, but softer. For a second Tal thought he caught a hint of kindness in Crow's voice, as if he was sorry he'd shouted at Ferek.

"*Seven* Freefolk?" asked Tal. "That's all? Counting

Jarnil? What about the other Sharers of the Light? How many of them are there?"

Jarnil looked down and mumbled something.

"None left?" repeated Milla, who was the only one who had heard his words. "None at all?"

"There were only ever twelve of us," said Jarnil. "Thirteen if you count Ebbitt, though he was never formally in the group and sometimes I wondered... anyway, Rerem – your father – was one, Tal. After I... began my new life down here, I made contact with them. But then over the years, they disappeared, one by one. Rerem was the last to go. I'm sorry, Tal, but I am sure that like the others... like the others, he must be dead."

"No, he isn't," said Tal, shaking his head. "I asked the Codex. It said, *He is the Guardian of the Orange Keystone. It has been unsealed and so he does not live. Until or unless the Orange Keystone is sealed again, he does not live. If it is sealed, he will live again.*"

Tal took a deep breath and got to his feet before continuing, the words coming faster and more forcibly as he spoke.

"That's why I want to know what the Keystones are, and how they get unsealed or sealed. And I think Milla needs to know too, because there is something terrible going on, and we all need to sit down and talk because no matter whether we're Chosen, or Un... Freefolk, or Icecarls, or something in between, if the Veil is destroyed and the sun breaks through and shadows swarm in from Aenir, they'll kill all of us! We should be working *together*, instead of fighting and arguing and *helping* Sushin and the Aenirans take over!"

Tal's impassioned words had the strongest effect on Ebbitt. The old man stopped pacing as he spoke and stood taller and straighter than anyone had ever seen him stand. His Spiritshadow stood at his side, a regal companion. And Ebbitt spoke with a voice that Tal had not heard from him before, an assured and somehow noble voice, without the wandering and strange humour. For a moment, Ebbitt was once again the Shadowlord of the Indigo he had once been, a great man among the Chosen.

"Seven Keystones stand in Seven Towers, forming the foundation of the Veil," he pronounced. "Seven

Guardians hold the secrets of the Stones. My nephew Rerem was indeed the Guardian of the Orange Keystone, as was my brother before him. If the Codex has told Tal that the Orange Keystone is unsealed, then the Veil is indeed threatened. For if all seven of the Keystones fail, the Veil *will* be destroyed."

The room was silent after Ebbitt spoke. Everyone stared at him, even Crow. Ebbitt met their looks, unblinking. Then his eyes seemed to twinkle, and his gaze shifted to the ceiling.

The silence broke as he began to speak again, his voice softer, his stance already shifting. He seemed diminished, more like his everyday, eccentric self.

"Sun and shadows," he said. "Sun and shadows. The Veil may block the sun, but it cannot block the pride and greed of the Chosen. We should have obeyed Ramellan's Strictures and never returned to Aenir. Everything that will come we have brought upon ourselves."

"The Orange Keystone unsealed," echoed Jarnil. Beads of sweat had come up on his forehead. "Unsealed. My cousin Lokar was the Guardian of the

Red. She disappeared a year before Rerem and..."

Jarnil's face went white and his voice almost disappeared. He drank heavily from his cup of sweetwater, as if it might bring relief from some great fear.

"I have just had the most terrible thought," he whispered. "Twenty-two years ago, Shadowlord Verrin of the Indigo disappeared without a trace, just like Lokar and Rerem. He was the first Chosen to disappear without explanation for almost a hundred years. He was probably the Guardian of the Indigo Keystone. The first to go."

Now incredibly agitated, Jarnil leapt up and gripped Ebbitt on the arm.

"Twenty-two years ago, Ebbitt! That same year that the three Chosen overstayed in Aenir!"

Ebbitt gently pulled Jarnil's fingers away, but did not speak. He kept staring up at the Sunstone in the ceiling and Tal could hear him humming some soft and doleful tune.

"What about the Chosen who stayed in Aenir?" Tal asked.

"The only one who came back was Sushin,"

whispered Jarnil. "He never explained what had happened and disclaimed all knowledge of the other two. He was more than a month late returning, but he was not punished. Verrin disappeared soon after he came back. I would never have thought to connect them before."

"This is Chosen business," interrupted Crow, sneering. "You talk of the Veil being destroyed. What does that matter to the Freefolk? We have never seen the sun in your Towers, or in your private world of Aenir. Maybe it is good the Veil will be destroyed."

Milla looked at him angrily.

"You speak faster than you think," she said. "The Veil is a defence, a ship-wall against shadows. It is not just the sun that would be let in, but also the many creatures of Aenir who hate and fear us. They are the ancient enemies of all our people, and they will slay Freefolk, Underfolk, Chosen and Icecarls."

Crow shrugged, as if he could shake off Milla's words. But he did not speak and she could tell that he didn't want to admit that he heard truth in her voice.

"How is a Keystone unsealed?" asked Tal.

Jarnil wiped the sweat from his forehead and folded his hands together before he answered, a habit Tal remembered from the Lectorium. It meant that Jarnil didn't want to admit he didn't know the answer and would talk a lot to disguise that fact.

"While the secrets of the Keystones are kept only by the Guardians," Jarnil began, "I understand that certain lengthy rituals and incantations—"

"Balderdash," interrupted Ebbitt. "Also codswollop and shadowpoop. No one knows, except the six Guardians."

"Seven," corrected Jarnil, angry at being so rudely interrupted.

Ebbitt smiled and held up six fingers, closing each one in turn into his fists as he counted.

"Red, Orange, Yellow, Green, Blue, Indigo."

"And Violet," added Tal. He was used to Ebbitt's eccentricities and weird lapses of ordinary knowledge, but this was so obvious he was embarrassed for his great-uncle.

Ebbitt shook his head and smiled, a secret smile.

"The Violet Guardian is the heir of Ramellan," he

said. "Not the toe, not the ear, nor the fingernail, but the heir of Ramellan. The in-hair-itor."

"The Empress," said Jarnil. He seemed relieved. "Then we need not fear for the Veil so much. It would be truly terrible if Sushin and his cohorts already had the Violet Keystone."

"Why?" asked Milla.

"The Seventh Tower holds all the ancient secrets of Ramellan, all the devices and machines of the ancient magic," said Jarnil. "Whoever controls the Violet Keystone controls the Tower. Fortunately, while the Empress is obviously unaware of the machinations of her Dark Vizier, she would never entrust control of the Violet Keystone to anyone but herself. We can rest easy on that one Keystone at least."

Ebbitt held up an imaginary book and turned some imaginary pages. It seemed that he had no trouble seeing the book himself, because he traced the first line with his finger, reciting.

"'The Empress Kathild, first of her line, came to the throne of Ramellan in unusual circumstances. Controversy surrounded the death of Emperor

Mercur, and his funeral was irregular and rushed, with no lying in state, giving rise to talk that he had been hideously assassinated and the body was not fit to view.'"

"That's from Kimerl's *History*," protested Jarnil. "She was totally discredited years ago and the book banned. I fail to see any relevance in it or, may I say it, in you, Ebbitt. Really, anyone would think you were the one who came out of the Hall of Nightmares!"

"Talk, talk, talk," said Crow. "That's all that ever happens here. If the Veil is in danger, and all of us because of it, what are we going to do? And what's in it for the Freefolk?"

"I will take word to the Crones," said Milla. "They will know what to do."

"I think we need to take a look at one of the Keystones," said Tal slowly. He was still thinking it through. "Maybe if we can work out how to seal it again, it would bring back the Guardian. Or if we find one that's still sealed, we could take it away so Sushin couldn't get at it."

"I doubt if the Keystones can be moved," said

Jarnil. "Since they are part of the Towers and the Veil. But your plan has merit, my boy. If we can release even one Guardian, they can tell us what we must do. And the Empress would surely believe us if we had one of the Guardians to tell their story. Even against the Dark Vizier. But who will go and to which Tower?"

"I will go," said Tal. "To the Orange Tower, to free my father."

12

"That is ill thought," Milla protested. "Where is your battle sense? Sushin has already laid a trap for you with your brother as the bait. There will surely be other traps, and better ones now, laid around your father and your mother. You should seek a different Guardian in a different Tower."

"You will need help to reach the Tower," said Jarnil. "Crow—"

"Forget it!" interrupted Crow. "Like I said, what's in it for us? If we help the Chosen fix the Veil, then everything stays the same. You say the Aenirans will kill us all, but maybe they'll only kill the Chosen."

"You have a Sunstone," said Jarnil. "I have taught

you how to use it. Under the plan of the Sharers of the Light, you would become a Chosen. The Empress will be grateful if we save the Veil. I am sure you would be raised up."

"I don't want to be raised up!" Crow screamed. "I want *all* of our people to be free!"

Bennem made a sound deep in his throat and stood up, looking wildly from side to side. Crow immediately quietened and went to his brother's side, sitting the big man back down.

"I want us to be free," he continued, his voice quite soft. "No more Underfolk, no more Chosen. I will only help you save the Veil if you all promise to help free my people."

"I will take your words to the Crones," said Milla. "They will weigh them with the other news I bring. I can do no more than that."

Tal looked at Jarnil and Ebbitt. Jarnil was frowning, his face now as red as it had been white a few minutes before. He was obviously very angry with Crow. Ebbitt, on the other hand, was looking at Bennem. Tal looked too, meeting the man's soft, unseeing eyes.

"I don't know what I can do, and I won't help kill Chosen or anything like that," Tal said hesitantly, still looking at Bennem. "But if you help us, I will do what I can to... change things and make sure that the Underfolk become Freefolk."

Crow looked at Tal with suspicion.

"I suppose that's better than nothing," he said grudgingly. "But you'd better do what you say."

Milla drew the knife she'd taken from Gill and said, "Do you wish me to make the cuts for the swearing?"

"No," said Tal, looking away. "That's not the way we do things here."

Crow shook his head too.

"A bond without blood is a bond soon broken," warned Milla. "And Crow has not spoken his part of the bond."

Tal looked back and met Crow's eyes. He could not see the burning hatred he'd seen before, but neither could he work out what the older boy was thinking.

"I'll help you get to the Tower," said Crow, but he hooded his eyes as he spoke. "And seal the Keystone or whatever it is we have to do."

Tal nodded. He noticed that Crow had not mentioned helping him come back from the Tower. But perhaps that was simply an oversight, not a thinly shrouded threat.

"And you, old man?" Crow asked Jarnil. There was little respect in his voice now. "Are you still dreaming about good little Underfolk lining up to be tested and joining the Chosen?"

"No," whispered Jarnil sadly. "You were a good boy, Crow. I fear you will not be a good man. All I ask is that you help Tal now. As you say, I am too old and broken, and I can only hope that we will save the Veil and nothing worse will come to either of our peoples. Come, Bennem. It is time to rest."

"I will leave after a short sleep," said Milla. "If Gill will still guide me."

Tal looked at her. In all the talk about the Veil and the Keystones, he had forgot about Milla and her desire to return to the Ice. But he couldn't think of any way to stop her. Besides, a small part of his mind was telling him they might need the help of the Icecarls, though he was reluctant to admit that.

"We could use your help in the Tower," Tal said, as he desperately tried to think of something that would convince Milla she should not go. "That might be more important than telling the Crones."

"No," said Milla very firmly.

"What about if..." Tal said, racking his brains. It was his fault Milla had lost her own shadow. If she was punished – or punished herself later – it would almost be as if he'd killed her himself.

"What if the Crones want to know more?" Tal said, an idea suddenly coming to him. "I mean, they can talk to one another in their heads or something, can't they? So if one needs to come back here, you'll have to guide her."

"I can tell others the way," said Milla. "If a Crone comes, she will choose Shield Maidens to guide and protect her. I am not a Shield Maiden."

Only Tal caught the slight shiver in Milla's speech as she said "I am not a Shield Maiden". For a moment he thought he'd imagined it, but it was there, the only sign he had ever seen of Milla almost losing control. It was almost as if he had seen her cry, something she had never done, even when terribly wounded by the Merwin.

"I don't think we should be inviting anyone to the Castle," said Jarnil nervously. "While I'm sure Milla and her people mean well, I think the situation with the Veil is best left to us here to deal with."

Milla looked at him, and then around the room at the pitifully small gathering. There was Jarnil, an old man and, as he had said himself, broken by the Hall of Nightmares. There was Ebbitt, who was a force to be reckoned with, but not to be depended upon. There was Bennem, who looked like a mighty warrior, but was a permanent sleepwalker, trapped inside his own head. There was Tal, whom she half hated for what he had done, but who was as close to her as anyone had ever been, an alien brother who was neither predictable nor easily understood. But he was brave and had growing powers. There was Crow, whom she knew little about, save that his bitterness and anger boiled so hot that he was a danger to friend as well as enemy. There were the other four Freefolk, hardy and resourceful, but hardly trained warriors.

Taken together, they were little to pit against the

Sushin monster, his guards, Fashnek and who knew how many Spiritshadows.

"I think you do not know the true strength and nature of the enemy," said Milla to Jarnil. "The Crones will decide what the Icecarls must do. After all, it was not just your Ramellan that defeated the Aenirans so long ago. It was our Danir too. You should not fear our help."

But they would fear, Milla knew, and perhaps they were right to do so. She was fairly certain what the Crones would do when they heard the news of free shadows in the Castle and the unsealed Keystones.

They would summon every Shield Maiden, Sword-Thane and available hunter to the Ruin Ship. A great host of Icecarls would be gathered, with a single aim: to take control of the Castle and return all shadows to Aenir.

She doubted that any Chosen, whether under Sushin's sway or not, would let that happen without a fight.

Soon, there would be war upon the Mountain of Light.

Milla was not sure whether to be glad or sorry that she would have no part in it. By then, she would have long since paid the price of her failings out on the ice.

13

There were many beds to choose from in the Freefolk Fortress. Obviously there had once been many more people to sleep in them. But Tal was too tired to think about that. His wounded leg and the after-effects of the water spider venom still troubled him. He was able to stay awake only long enough to complain about the Freefolk's primitive toilet and washing facilities (a stinking privy and cold water) before collapsing gratefully into a bed that was superior to most of the places he'd slept in the last few weeks.

When he woke, ten hours later according to his Sunstone, Milla was gone, with Odris. Adras was also missing. Tal woke feeling strangely stretched, with a splitting headache. It took him a little while to realise that this was due to his Spiritshadow's absence.

Adras returned only a few minutes later, drifting dejectedly into the central courtyard around the well.

"Where have you been?" asked Tal grumpily. He was cross from his headache, and because Milla had gone without saying goodbye. He was also grappling with guilt. Milla's fate was entirely his fault.

"Following Odris," replied the Spiritshadow. "But I had to come back, because of this stupid connection between us. Ow!"

He stabbed at his chest with one great puffy finger, his third jab a little too hard.

"Did you see any guards or other Chosen?" asked Tal, rubbing his own chest. He'd developed a sympathetic pain there as well.

"No," replied Adras. "Only red glows, like a distant sunset."

"That's good, I guess," said Tal. "Hopefully

they've given up looking for us."

"Perhaps they have," said Jarnil. He came over to the well and used his good hand to scoop up a handful of water to splash on his face. "The Day of Ascension dawns just hours away and all Chosen will be preparing for the journey to Aenir."

"Hours away?" asked Tal. He'd lost track of the days since his initial fall from the Castle. Time also flowed differently in Aenir. He looked at his Sunstone. It was the second hour of the morning, still the middle of the night, at least above the Veil. "That's great! It will be so much easier to get to the Red Tower."

"Don't forget that the Spiritshadows remain behind," warned Jarnil. "Once I would have said they will stay close to their masters' bodies, but now I am not sure."

"Have you... have you thought of going to Aenir to get a new Spiritshadow?" asked Tal.

Jarnil shook his head.

"It would not be safe for me. Remember, all the Chosen think I am dead. Anyone who saw me would think I was a creature that had taken on the shape of Jarnil Yannow-Kyr, and they would blast me to cinders. Besides, I am not sure I could bind a Spiritshadow now."

Tal nodded. Adras nodded too.

"Crow and Ebbitt are preparing clothes and equipment for you," Jarnil continued. "Crow has decided that it is best if only the two of you attempt the Tower."

"What about me?" asked Adras.

"And you, of course, Master Storm Shepherd," said Jarnil. "I should have said three."

"Master Storm Shepherd! I like that," boomed Adras. "You should call me that, Tal."

Tal sighed. He was missing Milla and Odris already, though he didn't want to admit it.

"I'd better go and get ready," said Tal. "Where are they?"

Jarnil pointed. But before Tal could walk away, he gripped the boy by the sleeve and leaned in close to him.

"I know only what Ebbitt has told me of the Icecarls and that he gained from you," he whispered. "Are they as strong and warlike as

Ebbitt says? You see, I am not sure we have done the right thing in letting Milla take any news to them."

"They are warlike," Tal answered, his voice low. He bit his lip a little before continuing. "But they are also honourable. They helped me return to the Castle. Milla has saved my life several times."

"I know, it is hard to think of someone who has saved your life as an enemy," Jarnil observed. "But what do you think the Icecarls will do when they hear of a way into the Castle? Ebbitt tells me Milla came here for a Sunstone, that they are rare in the world beyond. I understand that there are many different bands or tribes. What if one of them sees us as a storehouse of riches to be plundered? Would they risk attacking us, even knowing of our superior magic?"

"I don't know," Tal replied slowly. "They might."

"We must be careful, Tal," Jarnil muttered. "These Icecarls are outsiders. While I am keen to raise up suitable Underfolk, they are at least Castle-dwellers. I want you to promise that if the right opportunity comes along, you will warn the Empress, or some safe Chosen, about the possible danger from Icecarls raiding the Castle."

"I'll think about it," said Tal. It was hard not to promise. He still reacted to Jarnil as if he were a Lector, and Tal a small boy. He felt like he should be bowing and giving light in respect from his Sunstone.

"Do so," instructed Jarnil. He let Tal go and stalked away, his bad arm fluttering at his side.

"Forget you heard that," Tal instructed Adras as they went over to the cottage Jarnil had indicated.

"Forget what?" asked Adras.

"Forget it." Tal shook his head.

"What?" asked Adras. "What?"

"Nothing!" shouted Tal. "Never mind!"

Adras snorted and shot up to hover over Tal. A moment later, shadow-rain fell harmlessly on Tal's head. He ignored it and opened the door. Adras stayed outside, rumbling.

Inside the cottage, or rather the large cellar room underneath, Crow was sorting through a collection of strange garments. Great-uncle Ebbitt was asleep in a hammock strung up across one corner, his Spiritshadow beneath him. As Tal came down the steps, Ebbitt and his Spiritshadow opened one eye each.

"Beware the voices of sensible men, who sing almost in tune and know all the words," said Ebbitt.

Tal scowled. Sometimes Ebbitt was as bad as Adras.

"Come over here and try these on," instructed

Crow. He sounded friendlier than he had in the past.

Crow passed him two sets of white robes. The first was light, probably the standard Underfolk wear, but the other set was made of a heavier, shinier material. Crow also gave him a long-snouted mask that had clear crystal eyepieces, and a pair of crystal clogs.

Tal put on both sets of robes. The outer ones were heavy and hot, as if the fabric did not breathe. The mask was like a giant rat's head, the snout easily as long as Tal's forearm. It had holes in the end, but most of the snout was filled with a spongelike material.

"What is this?" asked Tal, before he slipped it on. The mask fitted very tightly to his face and under his chin, and was secured behind with adjustable straps.

"Filter mask," Crow replied. "We're going to be disguised as caveroach sprayers. The masks keep the poison out. Put these gloves on too."

Tal put on the long, almost transparent gloves. They came up to his elbows and were made of something like the gut of an animal. He was flexing his fingers and being thankful that they were so light when Crow threw him huge, heavy gauntlets made of the same material as the robes.

"Do we have to wear all this stuff?" Tal asked, his voice muffled behind the mask.

"Yes," said Crow. "The caveroach sprayers do all the corridors while the Chosen are away in Aenir. We will be able to get right up to the base of the Red Tower. But we'll have to spray on the way so we don't look suspicious."

"Your great-uncle thought of the disguise," Crow added reluctantly, nodding at Ebbitt. "It might even work, since he says your Spiritshadow can change its shape enough to be a normal shadow."

"Yes," said Tal. He hadn't really thought about it, but being a Storm Shepherd, Adras was much more malleable than any normal adult Spiritshadow, which had to basically conform to its Aeniran size and shape.

"I always wanted to be a caveroach sprayer," said Ebbitt from his hammock. "But I was doomed to a career as a Chosen."

Both Crow and Tal frowned at him, though for

different reasons. Since Crow had just put his mask on to adjust it, Ebbitt couldn't see either boy's expression and continued.

"I have often wondered where I might have ended up if I'd been a caveroach sprayer."

"Dead, like most of them," said Crow, taking off his mask. "Even with the suits, the poison gets them after twenty or thirty years."

"Why don't they change jobs?" asked Tal innocently.

Crow stared at him.

"Underfolk can't *change* jobs," he said scornfully. "We get written into the records when we're born. If you're a boy, you get your father's job. If you're a girl, you get your mother's. We don't even have names in the records. Just 'born to Sweeper #1346, a son, Sweeper #3019'. We make up the names later."

"Who keeps these records?" Tal was puzzled. He'd never heard of Chosen doing something so much like work, or of Underfolk having numbers instead of names.

"We do it to ourselves now," said Crow, his lip

curling into a sneer. "The Fatalists. The Chosen started it long ago, and the Fatalists are so convinced we are here only to serve that they just keep doing everything as it has always been done. Are you ready?"

The sudden question surprised Tal. He stammered out a yes.

"We'll go then," said Crow. "It'll take a few hours to get up to Underfolk Seven. We'll have to pick up some poison sprayers on the way."

"We're going right now?" asked Tal. "What about the others—"

"They've gone to get the airweed and scrounge for food. The sooner we get this over with, the better. That Milla had the right idea. No waiting around. I reckon she'd be a good looker too, once she washed up."

"What?" asked Tal. He'd never had time to spare any thought to what Milla looked like. He was confused about how he felt about her. He'd just got used to the guarded enmity between them, which was better than when she'd wanted to kill him.

"Milla," said Crow, twisting his face into an

exaggerated leer. "I wouldn't mind—"

"She'd kill you," said Tal.

"She liked me," said Crow. "I could tell. You'll see, when she comes back."

"She won't be coming back!" Tal burst out. "After she tells the Crones what she knows, she's going to give herself to the Ice! She'll be dead."

"What!" exclaimed Crow. In his surprise he dropped his odd expression. "Why?"

"It's complicated," muttered Tal. He picked up his mask and headed for the steps. "Are we going?"

"After you," said Crow.

But Tal was stopped at the bottom of the steps by Ebbitt's Spiritshadow. It stood in front of him and yawned, exposing a great mouth of shadow-teeth.

"Tal."

Ebbitt sounded unexpectedly serious. Tal went across to the hammock, while the maned cat stood aside so Crow could climb up and out.

"What is it, Great-uncle?" asked Tal.

"A caveroach does not know the difference between right and wrong," instructed Ebbitt, "because they have only instinct to act upon. You, on the other hand, have at least some small parcel of thought. Do not be a caveroach."

"What does that mean?" asked Tal. "Do not be a caveroach?"

"It's dangerous to be a caveroach," said Ebbitt. "Particularly when travelling in the company of a caveroach sprayer."

Tal nodded and wondered what in Light's name Ebbitt was going on about.

"The Icecarls cometh," said Ebbitt. "Unless I miss my guess. It's a pity you lost the Codex."

"It's here somewhere," Tal protested. "In the Castle. Maybe it will find you."

Ebbitt brightened at this thought.

"You think so?" he said. "It would be nice to chat to the old thing again."

"Goodbye, Uncle," said Tal. He bent down and hugged the old man, as usual surprised by Ebbitt's lightness. He was more fragile than he appeared.

"Goodbye, Tal," said Ebbitt. As Tal started to straighten up, Ebbitt whispered in his ear, "Bring me back a cake. One of the ones made with almond meal and boiled oranges. And change your mask before you go."

Tal nodded.

"I will, Uncle," he said. "In return for that cake – can I have two doses of the water spider antidote? In advance?"

15

Aided by the airweed and Gill's guidance, Milla found the entrance to the heatway tunnels without trouble. Gill wanted to continue on with her, but the Icecarl sent her back and waited to make sure she did not follow. Milla knew that she was the only one who knew the way through the heatway tunnels, and that was how she wanted it. Tal would not remember the twists and turns, and she was fairly confident he had lost the miniature map carved on bone – though there was a slim chance Crow had taken it, when he had found them unconscious the first time.

Odris followed the Icecarl silently through the

heatway tunnels, practising being a normal shadow, as Milla had instructed. Even though Odris had more freedom to change shape than a bound Spiritshadow, it was still difficult for her, particularly staying smooth. She was naturally puffy, and her arms and legs had a habit of billowing out to be much wider than they should be.

Milla kept her Sunstone low, so there was not quite enough light for Odris to feel entirely well. Being a natural shadow was further complicated by the coil of rope Milla had wrapped around her chest, and the extra blankets and gear she was carrying rolled up in a swag across her back. It all changed her silhouette and Odris had to pay constant attention to match it.

At the skeleton where Milla and Tal had found the Sunstone they now each had part of, Milla stopped and collected the skull and bones, wrapping them in a blanket. She felt that she owed the Chosen that much, for her Sunstone. She would take the bones with her and give them a proper Icecarl funeral, leaving them out in the clean snow and ice of the mountainside.

As she collected the bones, something glinted in the light. For a second Milla thought it was another Sunstone, put to sleep as the previous one had been.

It wasn't. It was an artificial fingernail, made of the same Violet crystal the Chosen used so extensively in the Castle. As Milla held the nail close, she saw it was flecked with tiny Sunstone fragments that picked up the light of her stone and sent it sparkling in currents through the nail.

The nail could be slipped on and was held securely by a thin band of crystal behind it. Milla tried it on. At first it was loose, then the band tightened. Milla tried to take it off, but it would not budge.

Milla shrugged. More Chosen magic. At least the nail was sharp and could be a useful weapon. Besides, she was already doomed by the Spiritshadow that loomed behind her.

"What is that?" whispered Odris.

"A nail," said Milla. "Remember, you must not talk once we are outside. An Icecarl might be hidden nearby. I will be slain out of hand if anyone suspects you are a Spiritshadow – and I must take my warning to the Crones before I die."

"All this talk of dying," said Odris. "I won't let you, you know."

"The Crones will deal with you," said Milla roughly.

"Hmmph," said Odris. "We'll see."

Just before the exit, Milla found her heavy fur coat, the new one she had been given at the Ruin Ship. She rearranged her equipment to put the coat on and looked down at Tal's coat that had lain underneath her own. She felt a vague uneasiness as she thought of the Chosen boy. It was rude to sneak away without a farewell, particularly from a Quest-brother – even if he had doomed her, giving away her shadow.

"Was that Tal's?" asked Odris. "You know, I feel like I miss him as well as Adras. Funny, isn't it? The feeling must be coming from you, because I don't care for him."

"It isn't," snapped Milla. "Tal is of no importance. Now be silent."

The cold hit her as they climbed out of the

tunnel entrance. Milla had never left the cold for long before and now it cut into her, taking her breath away. She had to stop and practise a Rovkir breathing exercise to stop shivering. Fortunately, the weather was fine, at least by Icecarl standards. The wind was strong and steady, and her Sunstone shone brightly out into the permanent darkness. No snow, hail or sleet fell into the circle of light around her.

Outside, Odris found it even harder to remain a natural shadow. The wind called to her, as it did in Aenir, tempting her to launch into the air and go with it. At the same time, she felt Milla's shadow deep inside her, anchoring her to the Icecarl girl. Somehow Milla's Rovkir breathing also helped the Spiritshadow keep control of herself.

It only took a moment to unwrap the skeleton and cast the skull and bones out into the dark void. With good fortune, Milla thought, something would find them useful, to chew upon or to line a lair.

Just below the entrance to the heatway tunnels was the blue crystal pyramid of Imrir, and past that, the gap in the road. Tal and Milla had jumped across it, coming up. Now Milla stood on the edge, staring down into the darkness.

She considered jumping across. Would it be weakness or strength to have Odris fly her over? She should not use her unnatural shadow. But it was her duty to get the Sunstone back to the clan as quickly as possible and warn the Crones of the danger to the Veil.

She had made the mistake of putting her own wishes ahead of her duty before, Milla thought.

She would use Odris.

"I want you to carry me across," Milla said, holding up her arms.

"I'll need more light," said Odris. "And a run up."

Milla nodded and backed up. She concentrated on her Sunstone as she walked. She was getting better at controlling it, but was still much slower than Tal. The stone slowly brightened, the ring of light around her expanding. Odris slipped up into the air and spread out into a puffy shadow-cloud, swaying in and out of the light as she adapted to the breeze.

Milla held up her arms again.

As Odris gripped her, a terrible, penetrating scream startled both of them. Odris lurched forward, even as a huge winged creature came down and thrust its claws through the Spiritshadow and almost into Milla.

"Perawl!" shouted Milla, but Odris held her so tight she could not draw her knife, or even turn and bite. She was totally defenceless and under attack by one of the most vicious predators on or above the ice.

16

Tal was surprised by how the Castle was transformed by the Day of Ascension. With all the Chosen retiring to their rooms to lie down and transfer their spirits to Aenir, and their Spiritshadows going with them, the Castle was left largely to the Underfolk.

It was eerie and still in the corridors. Tal couldn't help but think of what he should be doing. He should be with his family in their quarters lying down on his bed with the specially embroidered cover, waiting for his father to stand over him with his Sunstone, to guide him in the crossing.

He had never felt so alone.

It was strange to see so many Underfolk about too. They chose to use this time in a sudden frenzy to get to work on all the major and intrusive jobs of maintenance, repair and construction that could not be done while the Chosen were up and about.

Even down on Underfolk Seven, where Tal and Crow stopped to get backpack sprayers of cave-roach poison, there was considerable bustle and preparation. Underfolk storepeople were issuing tools and paint, lumber and screws, brushes and mops, replacement pipes and fixtures, and all manner of other things, to a steady stream of men and women.

As Crow had said, these Underfolk – Fatalists as he called them – seemed very keen to get on with their work. Tal would have thought they would use the opportunity of the Chosen's absence in Aenir to have a rest. But there was no sign of this. They were totally focused on their tasks.

Tal and Crow wore their masks, and Tal noticed everyone gave them a wide berth. Obviously Crow had not exaggerated about the poison. It seemed the other Underfolk feared to touch even the clothes of the caveroach sprayers, and perhaps because this embarrassed them, did not look at Tal or Crow either.

This was just as well, Tal thought, because Adras was having trouble being a natural shadow. He was always a bit behind, so that when Tal turned a corner, his shadow would keep on going for a moment and then hastily correct itself. No one seemed to have noticed so far, but it was making Tal very anxious.

Still, as long as they stayed out of the Chosen's individual chambers, or some of the specialised areas like the Imperial antechambers, where Chosen slept and their Spiritshadows guarded both them and the rooms, Tal and Adras should be safe from recognition.

It took nearly the whole day to climb up from Underfolk Seven to the highest level of Red, where they could begin the climb to the Red Tower, though it was also possible to get to the Tower from some of the higher colour levels. Normally Tal would have taken less than an hour to climb the steps and ramps, but they had to stop all the time and climb into drains or pipes or other out-of-the-way places to spray for caveroaches.

After a while, Tal noticed that Crow was watching him as they sprayed, almost as if he expected something to happen. Tal watched him too, mindful of Ebbitt's advice to change the mask Crow had given him. But he wasn't sure if that was simply Ebbitt's usual weirdness, or because his great-uncle expected Crow to have picked a defective mask for Tal.

Certainly Crow seemed to be making an effort to be friendly. His verbal attacks of the previous day were gone, and when he spoke, it was simply to instruct Tal on how to spray, or how to act like an Underfolk. Maybe his watching was also only to make sure Tal was staying in character. Maybe Crow wasn't waiting for him to suddenly pass out and die from the poison.

Tal couldn't make up his mind either way, but he decided to be careful.

From the High Red Commons, the huge chamber that in other times would be full of Chosen of the Red Order meeting to gossip and socialise, Tal thought there would be a stairway that led both to the foundation room of the Red Tower, and a narrow walkway that ran outside around the base of the Tower.

When Tal had climbed the Red Tower before, he'd started higher up in the Orange levels on a similar walkway, then climbed down and across to the Red walkway, where he had launched his assault on the Red Tower.

Though he'd never been in the High Red Commons before, Tal was certain that the layout would be the same as the High Orange Commons. When he saw the huge chamber, he knew that he was correct. Though it was furnished differently, with many low loungers upholstered in bright red cloth rather than the individual crystal chairs of the Orange Commons, the stairway was in the same corner. No more than two stretches wide and without railings, it ran up into the ceiling high above. Like the one in the Orange Commons, Tal suspected it was hardly ever used.

"That's it," he said to Crow, pointing.

"Good," said Crow. He looked around, making

sure that the whole chamber really was empty. Then he shrugged off his backpack sprayer and put it carefully upright against one of the loungers. Tal did the same, then they both backed away.

"Don't touch your gauntlets after they're off," instructed Crow. He showed Tal how to loosen both of them and then shake them off, rather than taking one off and then wondering what to do with the other.

They left the gauntlets and retreated again, to kick off their clogs and remove their outer robes. The lighter robes underneath were soaked with sweat and very clammy. Both boys had knives scabbarded on their sashes, and Tal wore his Sunstone ring openly.

Any Chosen or Spiritshadow that saw them would know instantly that they were some kind of enemy.

"Can I stop being a stupid regular shadow now?" asked Adras plaintively as Tal headed for the steps. The Spiritshadow lifted his head up as he spoke, though he kept Tal's basic shape. It looked very strange, as if Tal's shadow had somehow got curled up.

"When we're outside," Tal promised.

As they climbed the steps, Crow suddenly asked Tal a series of questions about the Keystones.

"Did your father ever tell you about how these Keystones work?" Crow asked when they were halfway up.

"No," Tal replied. His leg was hurting him again. The steps were steep and it would be easy to fall off. He needed all his concentration.

"I mean, this Guardian job seems to get passed on down the family. He might have mentioned it."

Tal shrugged and shook his head.

"What about old Jarnil's notion that they can't be moved? Do you think he's right?"

"I don't know." They were almost at the top. The door was probably locked, but Tal could melt the lock with his Sunstone. He'd stolen the key to the Orange door, but had long since lost it.

"They had to be put there in the first place," muttered Crow. "I bet they can be moved. We should take it away, so we're the ones who can use it."

Tal ignored him, pausing to get his breath back before he tried to open the door.

It was barred on the inside, but the bar came free easily enough. Tal leaned it on the steps and tried the door again. It was locked.

"I'll open it," said Crow, as Tal peered at the lock and the gap between the door and the door frame. "Let me past."

In his eagerness to get at the door, Crow pushed Tal slightly and the Chosen boy had to grab the iron staple that had held the bar to avoid falling off. It was a long way to the bottom, far enough to be fatal, and Tal knew Adras probably wasn't smart enough to have caught him if he fell.

But the push had seemed accidental.

"Oh, sorry," said Crow. Tal retreated a few steps down as Crow pulled a ring of keys out of his sleeve pocket and selected one to put in the lock. Then he inserted a strip of thin metal as well, and turned both of them.

The lock turned easily and the door swung open.

The light from the Sunstones in the chamber spilled out, but was swallowed by the darkness beyond. A freezing wind blew in, rattling the door and sweeping back the two boys' hair, stinging their faces and eyes.

Crow seemed paralysed. He stood there, his keys in his hand, staring out into the eternal night beyond the narrow walkway.

"Welcome to the Dark World," said Tal.

The Perawl shrieked again and took off, its prey in its huge claws. Unfortunately, Odris had made herself quite solid in order to hold on to Milla, so the huge, leathery flying creature could easily grip her shadowflesh.

"Ow!" cried Odris. "Ow! Ow! Ow!"

The Perawl couldn't really damage her, but its great talons were ripping her body and it hurt.

"Drop me!" shouted Milla. "Drop me now!"

They were still above the road, but the Perawl could swing away at any time, out into open space.

Odris obeyed, but a fraction too late. Milla saw the gap in the road below her, the deep crevasse she had jumped across before. She made a frantic grab and just managed to grip on to the little finger of Odris's left hand.

The finger stretched and stretched into a long rope of darkness as Milla swung below her Spiritshadow. The Perawl beat its mighty wings, taking Odris higher.

Milla focused on her Sunstone, brightening it as fast as she could, and at the same time she screamed, high-pitched and loud. Perawls couldn't stand very bright light or very loud, high noises. They didn't see or hear like any normal creature.

The Perawl gave a surprised squawk and tried to let go. But its talons were actually embedded in Odris and the Spiritshadow couldn't make herself more insubstantial without making her finger the same.

Milla fell. The Spiritshadow's finger got thinner and thinner, until it was burning through Milla's gloves, and she had to take one last swing and let go.

Immediately Odris thinned herself, slipping off the Perawl's talons like water. But she was already high above Milla. All she could see was a falling light, which was all too soon extinguished.

With the absence of light, Odris immediately grew weaker. She fell from the talons, but did not have the strength to fly. Instead, she plummeted straight down, a blot of formless shadow, indistinguishable in the darkness.

Milla missed the gap in the road by a few stretches, but the impact was hard. She tried to get up straightaway, but the wind had been knocked out of her, so she could only rise to a crouch. She could hear the Perawl squawking in the distance, but there was no sign of Odris nearby.

She could feel her Spiritshadow though. The connection between them was strong. Milla concentrated on getting her breath and tried to focus on the direction of the feeling.

It came in waves, a horrible, wrenching sensation, accompanied by feelings of weakness and nausea. Milla turned in a circle, to pin it down. After a few turns, she realised that Odris was further along the road and down quite a long way.

Milla also felt that the Spiritshadow wouldn't last much longer without light. Already she was fading, and as her strength faded, so did Milla's.

The Icecarl girl forced herself fully upright and started down the road. The smell of the ghalt, the molten stone used in the road, was strong. She drew it into her nostrils, regretting the loss of her face mask for a moment. Then she moved at a steady lope, much faster than she had climbed up with Tal.

She risked a fall going at such speed, but with every passing breath, she felt Odris fading. If she didn't get to her to provide light soon, the Spiritshadow would die – and from the feel of it, would take Milla with her.

That must not happen before she brought her news to the Crones, Milla thought.

She *must* get to the Crones.

Milla felt another wave of nausea and weakness hit her, and shuddered. It was a familiar feeling, as if the blood were flowing out of her body. Unconsciously, she held her hand to the Merwin-horn scar in her middle, as if to staunch the wound there. But it was healed.

Grimly, Milla increased her pace, leaping over

snow-covered stones and irregular chunks of ice. At the same time, she began to breathe the Tenth and Final Rovkir Pattern. The Dead-Walking.

That Pattern was the last resort and few Icecarls had the mastery of it. The Dead-Walking would enable her to keep going, no matter how wounded or weary, till her task was finally done.

Then she would die.

Lost in the Tenth Pattern, she did not even feel the falls, the tumbles and the many small bruises and cuts, as she continued to run pell-mell down the road. There was only the breathing and the constant pull of Odris's slow fade to nothing.

Odris felt the light before she saw Milla. It brought her back from somewhere where she had no thoughts, no feelings. In one moment she was falling from the Perawl, in the next, lying spread across the snow. As the Sunstone drew nearer, Odris felt her shape returning. Her shadowflesh flowed back to her like a tide, from where it had been spread across many stretches.

But Milla didn't really stop when she reached Odris. She paused and reached down. Odris grabbed her hand. The Spiritshadow hardly had a moment to shout hello before Milla ran on, dragging Odris with her.

"Slow down," shrieked Odris, as Milla fell down the far side of a large rock and nearly went over the edge. "You'll hurt yourself."

Milla didn't answer. She kept on running.

Odris flowed up her arm and twisted her head around to have a look. Milla's eyes were glazed and there was a strange light in them, reflected from the Sunstone burning brightly on her outstretched hand.

"I don't like this," whimpered Odris. "What are you doing?"

She heard no answer, but in her head came the sudden echo of Milla's thought.

The Ruin Ship and the Crone Mother. The Ruin Ship and the Crone Mother.

They came to a point where the road switchbacked ahead. Instead of running around the hairpin turn, Milla plunged over the side, sliding down thirty or forty stretches through snow, ice and stone.

"No, no, no!" shouted Odris. She puffed herself up and lifted Milla, so the girl swooped down instead of sliding. But this only encouraged the Icecarl. She left the road again and launched herself into space, to go straight down the mountain.

"Stop!" shrieked Odris, as she spread herself out to get the best glide and lift, exerting all her strength against the winds that threatened to dash them back into the mountainside. "Whoa! Milla!"

The Ruin Ship and the Crone Mother...

18

Tal and Crow stood on the narrow walkway, high up on the outside of the Castle. Adras flew above Tal, and above him loomed the huge Red Tower. Beams of light in all shades of red sprang from its many windows and openings, weaving a complex pattern in the sky. Behind it were the other six Towers, all of them taller, each also casting light out into the darkness.

Below them, other lights twinkled in the main bulk of the Castle. But even all these lights could not compete with the essential darkness of the world beyond. The Veil lay heavy on the world, and the light of the Seven Towers and the Castle spread only a little way.

"I didn't think it would be so cold," Crow whispered as he looked out on the darkness. "Or so…"

His voice trailed off. Then, with an obvious effort, he tore his gaze away and looked up at the Red Tower they were about to climb.

As Tal had found before, there were many spikes, gargoyles and strange ornaments that could be used as hand- and footholds. Even so, it was not an easy climb and would be impossible if they were not protected against the cold.

Tal concentrated on his Sunstone and soon warmth was flowing from it, along his arm and then all over him.

"You have a Sunstone," Tal said guardedly. He still wasn't sure about the wisdom of an Underfolk having a Sunstone. "Do you know how to warm yourself with it?"

"I know more than that," replied Crow. He took out his knife and flicked open the thin cover on the pommel, to reveal the Sunstone there. He concentrated on it for a moment and Tal saw it flash in answer.

"Ah," said Crow. "That's better. Do you want to go first, or shall I?"

"You go first," said Tal warily. "It will take us a few hours to reach the Veil. Watch out for the windows. Some are open and there may be Spiritshadows there."

Tal was very much aware of the danger. He could remember his first climb too well, and his brother, Gref, being taken through just such a window.

That climb seemed very long ago, but it was only a matter of six weeks or so. His entire life had changed that day, and not positively. Hopefully this climb would mark a change for the better.

At least this time he had a Sunstone, Tal thought. He looked at Adras, hovering above him. And a Spiritshadow of his own.

Once again, he was reminded of his first climb. There was a chance the Spiritshadow that had thrown him off would still be there, though if he was lucky, it would be guarding its master's body while he or she was in Aenir.

The Keeper, it had called itself.

Crow started to climb, easily pulling himself up

on to the first gargoyle's broad back. Tal let him get a bit ahead as he thought about the Keeper. Maybe it was a free shadow...

"Are you coming?" asked Crow. He was already a good twenty stretches up.

"Yes!" Tal called out. He started to climb, then stopped and spoke quietly to Adras.

"Adras. Keep a lookout and make sure you catch me if I slip."

"Sure," Adras replied. "What about thingummy? Do I catch him too?"

Tal hesitated.

"Yes," he said finally. "But make sure I'm safe first."

The climb went faster than the first time Tal tried it. Crow was quick, and Tal himself felt stronger and more confident. It only took them an hour to reach the Veil.

Tal had been ready to call out to Crow to stop, to prevent the older boy climbing up into the thick layer of ultimate darkness. But Crow had stopped of his own accord. He was crouched on a gargoyle's head, slowly raising his hand, watching it disappear into the Veil. With his arm apparently ending in a stump, he tried to play light on the Veil from his Sunstone, but the light simply stopped when it hit the dark barrier.

"It feels weird," said Crow. He was unable to suppress a shudder as he withdrew his hand. "What's up above?"

"Sunlight," said Tal. "There may be a Spiritshadow. A big one. It calls itself the Keeper."

"It spoke to you?" asked Crow. "Isn't that unusual?"

"Yes," replied Tal. He didn't mention that he suspected the Keeper was a free Spiritshadow.

"So how do we get through the Veil? Is there some secret... some Chosen secret to it?"

He couldn't quite keep the sneer out of his voice when he said "Chosen".

"Not as far as I know," Tal replied. "Just go quickly. I'll go first if you like."

"Good idea," replied Crow. "You can deal with this Keeper too. I don't mind watching."

"With your help, I hope," said Tal quickly. "We're in this together."

He was still never quite sure exactly what Crow meant. Was he joking?

"Adras, you'd better stay close to me," Tal ordered, as he edged up closer to the Veil. "Grab hold of my sash and hang on. You'll probably... not like the inside of the Veil."

"Why?" asked Adras. He drifted closer and hooked two puffy fingers through Tal's blue sash.

"It's made of absolute darkness," said Tal. "So dark you feel like you will never see the light again."

Adras was silent. Tal could feel him struggling with the concept of absolute darkness. Clearly it was beyond his imagination.

"Wait a minute or two and then come after me," Tal told Crow. "Climb through as quickly as you can. It probably helps to take a very deep breath before you start."

"Why?" Crow asked.

"I couldn't breathe last time," Tal explained. "I'm not sure you can breathe inside the Veil."

Crow raised an eyebrow, as if he didn't quite believe Tal. But he didn't speak.

Tal reached up into the Veil, watching his hands vanish. For a second he had the sensation that they had truly disappeared. He flexed his fingers in response and felt something he could grab hold of.

"Hang on!" he said. Then he took a deep breath and pulled himself up.

Into the Veil. Into the darkness.

It was a long way down the Mountain of Light. Odris kept shouting and screaming all the way down, even as she frantically steered them away from fatal gusts and sudden outcrops of stone.

Finally they hit the foothills, ploughing a trail through deep snow for at least twenty stretches.

Milla immediately got up to run again, but Odris held her fast.

"Milla! What's the hurry?"

Milla didn't answer. She began to drag Odris through the snow.

"Milla!" Odris tried again, this time stretching a hand around to slap the Icecarl in the face.

"Let me go," said Milla, her voice strangely flat. She hadn't stopped dragging the Spiritshadow. "I must go to the Ruin Ship."

"Something is really wrong with you," replied Odris. She kept hold of the girl and craned her head around again. Milla was breathing very strangely, her nostrils clamping in a curiously hypnotic pattern.

Odris was about to pinch Milla's nose shut when someone else shouted Milla's name.

"Milla!"

Odris whipped back to pretend she was a natural shadow, but it was too late. An Icecarl stood in the snow only a dozen stretches away, already kicking off her skis, her knife in her hand.

"Abomination!"

The Icecarl leapt at Milla, knife flashing at her throat. But Milla dodged and the knife raked across her shoulder, cutting fur and the skin beneath.

"To me!" shouted the Icecarl. It was a woman, Odris realised. Through her mental connection with Milla she felt a name swim into her consciousness.

Arla. Shield Mother.

Answering shouts came out of the darkness, from not far away.

Arla struck at Milla again, but the younger girl blocked the blow and threw Arla over her shoulder. The Shield Mother somersaulted in the air and landed on her feet, twisting to block Milla's strike in turn.

"I must reach the Ship, the Crones," said Milla in her strange, flat voice. "The Ruin Ship, the Crone Mother."

"Never!" spat Arla. "Shadow-slave!"

There was another quick exchange of blows as the two rushed together. Milla was cut again, across the thigh, but did not react to it. As Arla turned to attack again, Odris saw the Shield Mother was cut on the side of her face, where a blow had knocked off her face mask.

"Stop!" boomed Odris. She rushed in and gripped Arla with one hand and Milla with the other, both around the neck. "There's something wrong with Milla. She needs help, not killing."

"To me!" shouted Arla again. "Abominations!"

Milla said nothing, but lunged forward with her

left, supposedly empty hand. But the strange fingernail she wore suddenly extended, slashing through Arla's armour and furs.

Arla choked in midcall. Odris let go of her and dragged Milla back.

The Shield Mother tried to stagger forward, her knife raised. She only managed three or four steps before she collapsed. Dark blood flowed from her, stark against the pure white of the snow.

"To me!" roared Odris, in a fair imitation of Arla's voice. Then she let go of Milla and the girl was off and running immediately.

Odris followed her, wringing her shadow-hands with worry. Milla's mind seemed to have been affected by the cold or the darkness. It was still there, as far as Odris could tell, but was blocked off by this thick layer of thought that endlessly repeated the same thing over and over again.

The Ruin Ship and the Crone Mother.

Another Shield Maiden emerged out of the darkness, running at Milla. Odris swept forward and buffeted her out of the way, before Milla did something worse.

The Shield Maiden shouted some words that Odris didn't know, and the shout was taken up all around them, out in the dark. Odris could see and feel faint glows from weak lights all around, then she saw a sudden explosion of tiny green lights that shot up into the air. It would have been beautiful if it wasn't so obviously a signal.

It was followed a few moments later by the sudden blast of a deep horn, a horn being blown urgently, as if someone's life depended on it. A warning sound.

Still Milla ran on, always finding the hardest-packed snow or the roughest ice. She seemed to skim across the surface, bright golden light from her Sunstone flickering with her, her Spiritshadow flying at her side in her full Storm Shepherd size and shape.

The Shield Maidens and Shield Mother who had come bursting out of the Ruin Ship in answer to the alarm saw her running down the hill, but it was not Milla they saw. It was a monster, blood-soaked and phantom-lit, with a dark beast of shadow as its companion.

"Ready spears!" shouted the Shield Mother in charge. "Wait! Wait!"

Milla came on, Odris screaming at her to stop, her screams only making them both seem more terrible and dangerous.

"Wait!" roared the Shield Mother. Then, as the light from Milla's Sunstone spilled across the first rank of Shield Maidens, the leader dropped her arm and shouted.

"Throw!"

The crushing, breath-stealing darkness pressed down on Tal. He fought it as he struggled to climb, to find another handhold, to break free and into the light.

Just in time he remembered to close his eyes, so that when he burst out, he was not blinded. There was just the welcome flash of colour under his eyelids and the sudden warmth on his face.

Slowly, Tal opened his eyes a fraction and climbed completely out of the Veil, to sit astride a long bronze pole that thrust out of the wall.

Adras was still holding on to his sash. As the Spiritshadow came into the sun, he let out a surprised gasp, and then stretched and luxuriated in the sudden energy.

"I have missed the sun and the sky," he rumbled, far too loudly for Tal's comfort. "Look, there are clouds!"

There were many clouds in fact. It was close to sunset, and the sun was shining red and low through a deep band of cloud on the horizon.

Tal didn't look at the clouds for long. He was too intent on scanning the Tower above. There were no more gargoyles or stone ornaments, only long bronze rods and the golden nets that were suspended beneath the rods, nets that held neophyte Sunstones, Aeniran jewels that slowly absorbed power and light above the Veil.

Tal wasn't interested in them today. He was looking for the Keeper.

There was a balcony not far above. That was where he'd seen the Keeper last time. But it was empty now. Nor was there any sign of movement on the walkway even higher up.

Tal looked back down at the Veil. It was strange to see it spread right across the sky. It looked solid, like black soil, with the Red Tower growing out of it. If you didn't know what it was, you would never suspect that there was a whole world underneath.

Right at that moment, a hand thrust out of the Veil, fingers scrabbling frantically for a hold on the pole. Tal jumped with shock. Another, apparently disembodied arm followed, then Crow's head burst through.

His eyes were wide open. Tal had forgot to warn him about the sun.

Crow screamed and flung one arm across his face. His other hand lost its hold. Desperately his fingers flailed to regain it, as his body teetered backward.

Tal reached out and grabbed him around the wrist, and Crow gripped him with amazing, panicked strength.

It was too late. Crow was already overbalancing. He fell backwards. Tal let go, panicked himself, but Crow still kept hold.

Tal's own handhold slipped, his grip broken.

Together they fell into the Veil, even as Tal threw out his other arm, screaming for Adras.

They were in the darkness for only a fraction of a second. Tal felt Adras grab his arm with a familiar shoulder-wrenching suddenness. Then he was hauled back into the light. Crow came with him, almost wrenching his other arm out of its socket, until Adras reached down and pulled him up as well.

Both of them clutched at the bronze pole as if it were a long-lost friend. It took a few seconds before either of them spoke.

"You should have warned me!" hissed Crow. His eyes were still crinkled up against the sun. "It is so bright!"

"It's sunset," muttered Tal, in his defence. "Hardly that bright. Besides, I told you there was sun up here."

Crow muttered something angrily, but Tal couldn't catch what it was. He kept a wary eye on the Freefolk boy. At least Milla was predictable in this sort of circumstance, he thought. He didn't know what Crow was thinking at all.

"Well," Crow said finally. "Let's call it even, shall we?"

"Call what even?" asked Tal, puzzled.

Crow looked at him scornfully. "Don't give me that pretend stupid act. Who did you learn it from? Ebbitt?"

"I don't know what you're talking about," Tal said.

"Sure," snarled Crow. "Whatever you say. From now on, let's just help each other, all right?"

"I thought that's what we were doing. That's what I want to do."

Crow grunted. Carefully keeping one hand tight on the pole, he shaded his eyes and looked up.

"Darkness!" he swore. "What's that?"

Tal looked up swiftly and groaned. Sure enough, oozing over the balcony was the Keeper.

Tal still didn't know what creature it was in Aenir. The Keeper had a huge, grotesque head, with many eyes and a very wide mouth, full of hundreds of tiny, needlelike teeth. It's body was snakelike, long and sinuous, coiling along behind that horrible head.

It was bigger than Adras.

"Seek not the treasures of the sun," chanted the

Spiritshadow as it slid over the balcony. Its voice was high-pitched and screeching, awful to hear. "I am the Keeper and none may pass here, save those who know the Words."

Tal stared up at it, expecting at any moment to be totally consumed by the panic he had felt in his last encounter with the Keeper. But to his surprise he found himself quite calm. His hand was already coming up, his Sunstone glowing red as he instinctively prepared a Red Ray of Destruction.

"Adras, stand clear!" Tal ordered, his steady voice another surprise. "Crow, if you can do anything to this thing, do it!"

"I can if it gets close enough," said Crow. He was getting something out of the pouch on his belt, but Tal was too intent on the Keeper to see what it was.

The Keeper dropped on to the rod above them, twining itself around as it lowered its head for the next leap – straight on to Tal.

Tal kept concentrating on his Sunstone. He fed it anger and rage, and the Red grew deeper and stronger, swirling in the depths of the stone.

As the Keeper opened its too-wide mouth and

tensed to spring, Tal thrust his hand forward and released the pent-up power of the Sunstone.

A Red Ray too bright to look upon shot out, a thin spear of light that punched through the Keeper's head. Drops of shadow spurted out of the back of its head. It screamed and recoiled, in pain and surprise.

Tal's relief died as he saw the droplets of shadow leap from the bronze rod and the Tower wall and fly back into the Keeper. In a few seconds the hole drilled by the Red Ray had closed and the Keeper was once again preparing to spring.

"None may pass here!" hissed the Keeper.

"Can you hold it still?" shouted Crow. There was no need for shouting, but Tal understood why he was.

"No... yes... I don't know," he shouted back. "Adras, grab hold of that thing."

Adras had only been waiting for the word. He roared a battle cry and unleashed two bolts of shadow-lightning at the Keeper. More shadow-drops flew, then Adras was upon it, gripping it in a bear hug with his mighty arms. But its snake body was as quick to wrap around him and Adras grunted as the thing began to squeeze.

Its head lowered too, and it bit at Adras's shoulder. Adras howled, squeezed even harder and bit back.

"It's still moving too much!" shouted Crow. He was getting up on the bronze rod now, intending to climb up to the next one where the two Spiritshadows were wrestling and biting. He had a strange silvery bag in his left hand.

Tal stared down at his Sunstone. There had to be something he could do to immobilise the Keeper. A variation of the Hand of Light. A rope. Something! Anything!

21

As the spears flew, Odris leapt upon Milla, grabbed her, and glided with her only a half-stretch above the snow. The spears went overhead. Odris, with Milla tucked underneath, ploughed through the line of Shield Maidens. Knives cut at the Spiritshadow's back as she passed, but only sank into the shadowflesh and rebounded.

Odris kept going. Ahead of her, a huge wall of golden metal loomed, part of some giant structure that disappeared up into the darkness. There was a doorway in the side, with fuzzy green lights all around it.

"Ruin Ship, Ruin Ship," Milla repeated. Odris

understood that this metal house was Milla's target. Perhaps when she reached it she would come to her senses.

If she reached it. Odris felt several spears strike her in the back, some of them going far enough through her to at least scratch Milla. Even so, the Icecarl did not cry out.

Odris kept on gliding, as close to the ground as she dared, sometimes grazing it a little with Milla. Near the door, she swooped up, dropped Milla and turned to face their pursuers.

No more spears flew. Thirty or more Shield Maidens drew their long knives and rushed forward in total silence.

Odris drew herself up to her full height and shadow bolts of lightning formed in her hands. She was about to throw them when she heard a voice behind her call out a rapid sequence of strangely familiar words, followed by the shouted command, "Stop!"

The Shield Maidens stopped. Odris would have thrown the shadow-lightning, but she found herself unable to move. Whatever the words were, they had done something to the shadow in her heart, Milla's shadow. It had reached out and stilled her muscles.

Odris couldn't even turn to see who had spoken. Now all she could hear was Milla's voice. Milla was suddenly babbling on about the Aenirans and the Veil and Sushin and Odris and Adras, but it was all mixed up and it didn't make much sense.

The voice spoke again.

"Libbe! Go to Crone Dalim, ask her to come quickly with her medicines. Breg, go to the Mother and ask her for a shadow-bottle. Run!"

Odris kept trying to turn around. She could feel the shadow inside her going back to sleep, or whatever it normally did, and she was regaining control of herself. Slowly, she began to turn.

A silver-eyed woman in black furs was cradling Milla, her hand placed firmly on the Icecarl girl's heart. As Odris turned, the woman looked at her and rapidly spoke the same words again.

This time, they had less effect. Odris felt the shadow stir inside her, but it could not hold her. She turned completely around and took a step forward.

A glowing knife appeared in the woman's other

hand. A shorter version of the Merwin-horn sword Milla had lost when she had impaled Sushin.

"Come no closer, shadow," ordered the woman. "You shall not have this girl."

Odris sighed and sat down.

"I don't want to *have* her," she said.

The woman started and there was a gasp from the Shield Maidens. Apart from the ones who had run off, they were standing still, as the woman had commanded, in a ring around Odris, none closer than thirty stretches.

"You speak," said the woman. "It is long since we have seen a shadow that speaks."

"Is Milla all right?" asked Odris. "She feels sort of sick to me and she's been acting very strange."

"Milla?" asked the woman, looking down. "If that is her name, she has gone far into the Tenth Pattern. I do not know if we can guide her out. If we cannot, she will die."

"I don't want her to die!" wailed Odris. "What will happen to me?"

The Spiritshadow started to weep, huge shadow-tears rolling on to lie black upon the snow.

"Beware the stratagems of shadows," muttered the woman. "Lemel, you had best call the Mother Crone herself and not just a shadow-bottle."

"No need," said a calm, quiet voice. "I am here."

A very old, tall woman spoke. Odris saw that this one had strangely milky eyes. She walked forward with confidence, pausing to look down at Milla. Another Crone, younger and less bright-eyed than the one with the knife, followed her. She went straight to Milla, took something from the bag she carried and broke it under the girl's nose.

"Ah, I thought it would be Milla," said the Mother Crone. "She got her Sunstone, I see."

"She spoke of strange things," said the first Crone. "Words she had laid upon herself to deliver, dead or alive. I have them."

"Then I will hear them, in due course," said the Mother Crone. "Can she be saved?"

"If you wish it," said the younger Crone. "She is at the choosing of the ways."

"Bring her back," the Mother Crone instructed. "I think I will want more than a few words. Now, Speaking Shadow, what is your name and kind?"

"I am Odris, Storm Shepherd, once of Hrigga's Hill," said Odris. "Who are you?"

"I am the Mother Crone of the Ruin Ship," said the Mother Crone. "I am the Wisdom of Danir, the Living Sword of Asteyr."

"Oh," said Odris. She got up and bowed.

"No Aeniran is permitted upon the Dark World, by the ancient law of Danir," continued the Crone. "By what right do you come here?"

"I came with Milla," Odris explained. "She wanted to tell you about the Veil being in danger, and the Keystones being unsealed, and—"

"Stop!" ordered the Mother Crone. "We will speak of this with Milla herself. I say again, by what right do you come to the Dark World?"

"I don't know," said Odris miserably. "I just wanted to get away from the Hill and then I had to follow Milla."

"You must be taken for judgement," said the Mother Crone. "Will you go willingly to your prison or must I force you?"

Odris looked around. The Shield Maidens probably couldn't hurt her, though there was that

Crone with the glowing knife. The Mother Crone also seemed very confident Odris could be made to obey her.

"I'll do what you want, on one condition," Odris answered.

"We do not make conditional agreements," said the Mother Crone. "Yet you can tell me what you want. Perhaps it is not a condition after all."

"I want you to stop Milla from giving herself to the Ice."

The Mother Crone looked down at Milla. She seemed to be merely asleep now, breathing normally, as the younger Crone cleansed and bandaged her wounds.

"We cannot promise that," she said. "It is every Icecarl's right to go to the Ice. Besides, Milla herself must be judged. Perhaps our judgement will be that she must go to the Ice."

Odris frowned and shot up into the sky. But she knew she couldn't go very far from Milla. Even if she could escape that binding, there was no light out in the world. She would fade to nothing.

There didn't seem to be much choice.

"What is this prison?" she asked. "And the judgement? Will I get to speak my side?"

"Yes, you will be able to speak," said the Mother Crone. "And here is the prison."

She drew a tall bottle of golden metal out of her robes and unscrewed the stopper.

"I can't get in that," said Odris. "It's too small."

"I think you will be surprised," replied the Mother Crone. "Will you try?"

Odris felt a strange power in the old woman's voice. Power that was building, as if the next time she spoke, her words would fly out like a Storm Shepherd's bolts of lightning.

"Oh, all right!" she said.

The Mother Crone held out the bottle. Odris billowed down two legs and trudged over, her head downcast in defeat.

"Are you sure this is big enough?"

The Mother Crone nodded. Odris pushed a finger in the top, then another. Somehow she got her whole hand in, and arm, and then the rest of her was sucked in, like being caught up in a whirling storm.

Strangely, Odris did not feel cramped. There was even some light coming in from outside, so she did not feel sick. But when the stopper was screwed back in, Odris did get a strange feeling. There was the hint of other shadows here, from long ago. Shadows who had never been released, who had long since faded into nothing...

22

Tal concentrated on his Sunstone, willing Orange light to form. Dimly he was aware of Adras shouting and swearing, and the Keeper hissing, but he blocked them out. The Light was the only thing that mattered.

Slowly, he wove the Orange light out of the ring. It came out as a bright, narrow strand that thickened as it rose up. It became a rope, as broad as Tal's arm. He kept drawing more of it out, until it rose straight up above him for twenty or thirty stretches.

Sweat beaded on Tal's forehead as he concentrated on the end of the rope. He directed it into a loop, tying a slip knot. Then he gently lowered the noose of light down towards the struggling Spiritshadows.

The noose hung there, Tal holding it with his mind and his Sunstone, as he waited for an opportunity. It bobbed down a few times, but he never completed the cast. Adras always got in the way.

"I can't hold it," whispered Tal after the fourth attempt stopped suddenly in mid-air, as Adras swayed back under the noose.

"Adras!" roared Crow. "Push it away!"

Adras grunted. For a second he made no move. Then he suddenly let go and instead of hugging the Keeper, pushed it away. At the same time, Tal dropped the noose. It went perfectly over the Keeper's head. Instantly, Tal tightened it, the rope of light cutting deep into the shadowflesh. Then he quickly wrapped the rope around the rest of its body as Adras leapt free, pinning the Spiritshadow in place against the bronze pole.

"Quick! I can't keep it going!"

This was the moment Crow had waited for. He jumped to the higher pole and swung himself up in front of the struggling Spiritshadow. The bag in his hand was made of gold mesh and he slipped it over the Keeper's head, though it struggled to evade him.

"Let it go!" shouted Crow.

"What?" screamed Tal. "Are you crazy?"

The Keeper's head was in the strange gold-mesh bag, but Tal didn't see how that would help. It would just pull out and knock Crow off, before killing Tal and Adras.

"Let the rope go!"

Tal shook his head. But that had much the same effect. He lost concentration and the rope began to fade. Tal looked to Adras, ready for a quick getaway.

Strangely, the Keeper did not pull its head out of the bag. Instead it actually slithered further in. Crow held the bag open until all the Spiritshadow was inside, then closed the drawstrings tight and hung it over the end of the pole.

"Pity it's the last one," he said, sitting astride the pole and dusting his hands in the attitude of a man finishing a job well done.

"Last what?" asked Tal, staring at the bag.

"Shadow-sack," replied Crow. "We only had three.

Jarnil found them for us a few years ago, I don't know where. He wouldn't say."

"Can it get out?"

"Only if someone lets it out. Someone real. Shadows can't touch that golden metal. Didn't you know? I thought you'd get all this in your Lectorium."

"No," said Tal. "I'm only beginning to realise all the things I wasn't taught in the Lectorium."

"We'd best move on," said Crow. "That was a noisy fight."

He started to climb up to the next rod. Tal looked at Adras.

"Are you all right?"

"Hah!" boomed Adras. "I would have won. It was weak."

"I guess that means you are," Tal said. There were some holes in the Spiritshadow's shoulder, but he didn't seem bothered by them. Besides, Tal knew Spiritshadows healed very quickly under the sun. "Come on."

On the rod above, Crow had stopped to reach into the nets to fill his pockets with Sunstones. But he had picked up only a handful when he threw them down again.

"These aren't Sunstones!" he exclaimed angrily.

Tal joined him and picked up a handful himself. The stones were shiny black ovals, with only the slightest hint of inner fire.

"Sunseeds," he said, not admitting to Crow that he had never actually seen them before. "Jewels from Aenir. They must have harvested the ready Sunstones just recently and put these out to grow in power."

"Just my luck," grumbled Crow. "Let's hope the Keystone's still there."

He started climbing again, even faster than he had earlier.

"Anyone would think it's a race," Tal complained. Then he thought, *Maybe it is*. He didn't know what Crow really wanted up here or what he had really agreed to.

"A bond without blood is no bond," Tal muttered. He reached up to the next pole and swung up. "Adras! Give me a hand!"

It was a surprisingly long way to the top of the

Tower, almost as far above the Veil as it was below. With Adras's help, Tal caught Crow before too long, but night had fallen before the very pinnacle of the Tower was in easy reach.

They had been tempted to go on to one of the balconies or walkways and continue up the stairs, but caution had prevailed. So they had kept to the outside, the bronze rods and the nets of spun gold with their carefully arranged Sunseeds. Every now and then Crow had taken up a handful, just in case, but he had yet to find a proper Sunstone.

At last they came to the final bronze rod, half Tal's height below the topmost walkway. They could see the spire of the Tower, not far above, surrounded by a crown of distant stars. Light still spilled out above them, but not the bright red rays of the lower windows, just a dim, pinkish glow.

The Tower had grown slender at its peak, little more than forty stretches in diameter. Tal and Crow sat on the pole, listening, hoping to hear if anything was inside the room above. But all they heard was the wind and the soft rattle of the Sunseeds and the nets.

"There may be traps," said Crow. "I'd better take a look first."

"There may be," said Tal. "Light magic traps. We'd best go together."

Crow nodded. He crouched on the pole, hanging on with one hand as he reached up to the railing above, careful to put his hand between the sharp serrations. Tal moved up next to him and had to reach out further across. Adras hovered next to him and reached out a steadying hand.

Crow jumped. An instant later, Tal followed.

Tal and Crow landed on the walkway together. Both were scratched by the sharp railings, but not seriously. They stood carefully at the very edge of the narrow path and looked into the room in front of them.

The top of the Red Tower was a domed room, open to the air, with four arched doorways, one at each cardinal point of the compass, leading to the circular walkway. Inside the room, the ceiling was covered in a mosaic of tiny Red Sunstones, glittering like a seam of jewel-filled rock. The floor was tiled in red and white, but not in any regular or obvious pattern.

Hanging upside down – or perhaps growing – from the very centre of the domed ceiling was a tree of Red crystal. Its trunk was straight and bare for several stretches, before it branched out into a canopy that covered most of the room. Each branch had a silver bell on the end.

Tal stared at it, trying to figure out what it was for. There was a strange cluster of small silver hands around the base of the trunk, at the apex of the dome. They seemed to have some purpose... every hand held a thin wire that went back into the trunk of the tree.

"What is that?" asked Crow. He spoke quietly and pointed at the tree.

"I don't know," Tal whispered. His attention had been caught by what was under the upside-down tree.

On the floor of the room, there was a pyramid-shaped plinth of a darker red, about as high as Tal's chest. Two silver hands were mounted upon it, and between them was clasped a large, slowly pulsing Sunstone. It had to be the Red Keystone.

"I don't like the look of all those bells," said

Crow, studying them with a burglar's practised eye. "Or the silver hands."

Then Crow saw the Keystone. He started forward and stopped only a step from the doorway.

"Maybe you should send Adras in to get it," he suggested.

"Sure," said Adras, before Tal could speak. The Spiritshadow surged forward, but as he tried to enter the arched doorway, the Keystone flashed and a solid sheet of Red light slammed shut like a door. Adras bounced off it with a startled "Oof!"

The Red light faded as he bounced back and the Keystone was quiet once more.

"No Spiritshadows allowed," said Tal. "There must be other defences too."

He looked up at the tree and the bell-branches again, and then at the floor. The red tiles seemed to be placed in line with bells above them.

"I think the bells sound if you step on the wrong tiles," Tal said slowly, as he thought it out.

"Maybe," said Crow. "Let's see..."

He leaned forward and lightly pressed a white tile with his finger. Nothing happened. Crow pressed a little harder. Still nothing.

"Now the red," he said, transferring his finger to the closest red tile.

As his finger touched, a silver hand above twitched slightly and the bell above rang – a tiny, hesitant ring.

"So the red tiles sound the bells," agreed Crow.

They both looked across at the floor. The arrangement of the tiles seemed haphazard, but now they realised that it would be almost impossible to reach the plinth. The individual tiles weren't big enough to get more than most of one foot on, and the red tiles were cleverly distributed so that there were more of them the closer you got to the plinth, and the white tiles too far apart to stretch.

"There must be a way to silence the tree," said Crow.

Tal shrugged. "The proper words, or proper light. But the wrong thing would set them all going."

Crow looked up at the tree, then down at the floor, and finally at Tal.

"You're lighter than me," he said. "I reckon I can stand just inside on those two white tiles and boost you up to that branch. Then all you have to do is grab any bell that I might set off."

"That's all!" protested Tal. He looked at the crystal tree dubiously. If it was like the ones in the Crystal Wood, it would be quite strong enough to climb. But it would also be very easy to fall off it, or cut himself on the narrower branches.

"Do you have a better idea?"

"I could have another try," said Adras, who was still rubbing his head.

"No," said Tal. "I don't have a better idea."

Even without a better idea, they still walked around and checked the other three entrances, to see if either the tree or the floor looked different or easier to move across.

They didn't, so Tal, Crow and Adras returned to the western arch. The sun had set completely, but the walkway was lit by the Red light that spilled out from under the dome and through the arches.

The brightest light came from the Red Keystone. It shone between the silver hands on the plinth, pulsating with the uncanny and disturbing rhythm of a human heart.

One that was beating a lot slower than Tal's.

"Ready?" asked Crow.

Tal nodded.

Crow backed up to the arch and then stepped back, craning his head. Keeping his toe pointed, his foot just fitted within the confines of one white tile.

Both boys held their breath. But no bell sounded, no light flashed.

Crow stepped back with his other foot. For a moment it looked like he would lose his balance. He swayed and then recovered, cupping his hands so Tal could use them as a foothold.

Adras helped him, being careful not to step too close.

Held high outside by Adras, Tal put his foot in Crow's hands and ducked under the arch. Adras was still holding the back of his shirt.

"Now!" cried Tal.

Adras let go, Crow jerked his hands up and Tal pushed.

He went flying towards the ceiling and the closest branch.

It seemed further away than it had from outside.

Milla woke in a dream. She knew it was a dream because she was standing with one foot on the bowsprit of a speeding iceship, the wind whistling through her hair. Sunstone light spilled on the ground ahead, and the ship bucked and rolled as its runners met uneven ice.

Just ahead Milla could see a great roiling mass of Slepenish, breaking through the ice. Small icebergs bobbed and splintered as the millions and millions of Slepenish turned the ice into open sea.

The iceship was heading straight for the hole in the ice and certain destruction. Yet it was not too late for the ship to turn, if only a warning was given.

Milla tried to shout, but no sound came out of her mouth. She tried to wave her arms in warning, but they would not move.

She didn't mind meeting her end in the freezing water, but she didn't want to take a whole iceship full of her people with her. Even in a dream.

A hand touched her shoulder. With it came freedom. Milla turned, meeting a Crone's silver gaze.

The Crone nodded.

"Ware water!" Milla shouted. "Turn aside! Turn aside!"

She was still shouting the warning when she woke up.

The same Crone she had seen in her dream was leaning over her. Behind her Milla could see the golden sheen of the metal walls of the Ruin Ship.

She had made it and she wasn't dead. The Crone had brought her back.

"Do not try to get up," the Crone warned. "You were far gone in the Tenth Pattern. You will be weak for some days."

"I must tell the Crone Mother," whispered Milla. "Shadows. Aenir. The Veil."

"We know," soothed the Crone. "You told me while you were still in the Pattern. And we have walked in your mind while you slept."

Milla nodded. Now she was done. The Crones knew what they must know.

"I will go to the Ice," she said. "I have the strength for that."

The Crone shook her head.

"You may not go to the Ice. At least not yet. Both you and your shadow companion must first be judged, when you are strong enough to bear the weight of whatever judgement is passed."

"There is no need for judgement," said Milla weakly. "I lost my shadow. I brought a free shadow from the Castle and…"

She frowned as dim memories came swirling in.

"Did I fight the Shield Maidens?"

"Yes," said the Crone calmly.

"Arla…" whispered Milla. "I seem to remember…"

"The Shield Mother is dead," said the Crone bluntly. "She died with a knife in hand, as she would have wished. Yet perhaps she was always too ready with her knife, instead of words."

"I... I killed Arla?"

Milla's head fell back. She had only flashes of memory since emerging from the heatways. Now one fragment was clear in her head. The strange nail on her hand, sweeping across Arla's stomach.

"It was not a fair fight," she said, the words choking her. She raised her hand to show the strange, Sunstone-flecked fingernail of Violet crystal. "I had Chosen magic."

The Crone shook her head.

"It was not a trial combat, so why should it be fair? Besides, Arla was a Shield Mother, stronger and more experienced than you. And that strange nail is not Chosen magic."

"What is it?" asked Milla, her voice husky, already fading as she struggled to stay conscious.

"It is ours," said the Crone. "One of two made for Danir long ago. One she kept, and one she gave away. Both have been lost for more than a thousand circlings."

Milla heard the Crone's voice getting further and further away. She tried to answer, but could not. Unconsciousness claimed her.

*

When she came to, there were three different Crones in her room, and several Shield Maidens.

"The Crone Mother of the Ruin Ship has decreed you will be judged," said the eldest, milky-eyed Crone. "Are you strong enough to bear whatever your fate may be?"

Milla nodded. She was unable to speak and she couldn't look at the Shield Maidens. They clustered close as she shakily stood up, their hands on their knife hilts.

"Follow me," said the older Crone. She pulled back the curtain of furs and led Milla out. The other Crones fell in behind, but a Shield Maiden remained on either side of Milla.

It was a slow progress. Milla had never felt so exhausted. She could hardly put one foot in front of the other, but somehow she managed to keep going. The Shield Maidens stopped when she stopped, but at no time did they or the Crones offer to help her.

Finally they came to a wide door, the furs already pulled aside. The Crones went in with Milla. The Shield Maidens did not. They pulled the fur curtain across as soon as the last Crone passed.

Milla's eyes had been firmly on her own feet all the way. Now she slowly raised her head.

They had come to a huge room, as large as the Hall of Reckoning. But this room was almost empty, a great chamber of gleaming, golden metal walls, ceiling and floor. There were no Sunstones present, but hundreds of lanterns burning Selski oil were set in concentric rings around the single item of furniture in the whole hall – a tall chair of white bone, that stood in the centre of the room.

Milla was led to it and sat down. The two younger Crones tied her wrists and ankles to the chair with strips of Wreska-hide. The bonds were tight and the knots strong.

Milla did not resist.

Then the Crones turned the ring on her finger so she could not see the Sunstone, and retreated to stand against the walls.

Milla sat silently waiting. It was just her and the three Crones in the huge silent room.

She was too tired to wonder what would happen next. What could happen? She had brought a shadow to the Ruin Ship and she had slain a Shield Mother. They would probably use the Prayer of Asteyr on her and send her out to stand before the Selski Living Sea. Her name would become a curse, a word to be spat, a ballast-stone of loathing the Far-Raiders would have to bear for many circlings.

She had disgraced herself, her clan and her people. Now even a clean end of her own choice upon the Ice was out of her reach.

Milla closed her eyes and let her chin slip forward a little, a small sign of the despair within her.

Then she heard the curtain open and she looked back up.

Crones were entering the room. Many Crones, more than Milla had ever seen. Scores of Crones, from the bright blue-eyes of the newest to the milky-eyed oldest, all of them clad in black. They spread out along the walls, the only sound the shuffle of their feet and robes.

There were hundreds of them, Milla saw. Crones from every clan and ship. Perhaps even her own Far-Raiders' Crone was there.

Milla hung her head again, ashamed. She did not want to see the Crone who had always had such high hopes for her.

Finally the Crone Mother of the Ruin Ship entered. While all the other Crones lined the walls, she strode out across the open space, a tall figure, her shadow flickering by her side in the lantern light.

She stopped by the chair, unscrewed a bottle she had under her arm and laid it down next to Milla. Then she stood behind the chair and raised her arms high. There was total silence in the hall and all the Crones were still.

The silence lengthened. No one moved. Milla held her breath.

Finally the Crone Mother spoke, her voice soft, but echoing throughout the vast room.

"Today we decide the Doom of Milla of the Far-Raiders, daughter of Ylse, daughter of Emor, daughter of Rohen, daughter of Clyo, in the line of Danir since the Ruin of the Ship.

"Before that Doom is decided," the Crone Mother continued, "we must hear the words of Milla of the Far-Raiders. For she has brought evil tidings and the news she bears must be weighed with her fate."

"What... what must I say?" asked Milla.

"Everything," said the Crone Mother. "Begin when you left the Ruin Ship, with the Chosen Tal, in your quest for a Sunstone. Tell us everything."

Milla cleared her throat and slowly began to speak. She told the assembled Crones about the journey into the Castle, the skeleton with the Sunstone, Great-uncle Ebbitt and the attack by the guards, the Hall of Nightmares, the Mausoleum, the transfer to Aenir, the Storm Shepherds, Tal's use of the Prayer to Asteyr, how Odris was bound to her while she was unconscious, the riddling pool in the desert, the Dawn House, Zicka the lizard, Asteyr's ship, the Codex, Sushin and the Merwin-horn sword, the Keystones and the threat to the Veil... it all came tumbling out of her.

The Crones listened in silence, though occasionally a ripple passed through their ranks, as it did when she spoke of Asteyr's ship.

They listened, their strange blue or silver or cloudy white eyes intent on Milla. And as they listened, they judged.

25

Tal was afraid the bell would ring anyway as he gripped the branch. But it didn't. He swung a leg over and hauled himself up, grateful that the branch was round, without sharp crystal edges.

"That bell," said Crow, pointing to a branch a stretch or so away.

Tal balanced on the branch he was on and leaned across. He ran his hand along the branch to the bell and grabbed the wire that would make it sound.

"Ready," he said.

Crow nodded and jumped across. His foot fell on a white tile and partially on a red. As he landed, the wire twitched under Tal's hand, but he had it fast and the bell did not sound.

"That one," Crow said again, pointing.

"This one will sound as soon as I let go," protested Tal. He could feel the tension in the wire. Looking up, the silver hand at the base of the tree was still plucking mindlessly away.

"You can hold both," Crow assured him, without bothering to look.

Tal sighed and examined the situation. If he did the splits across two branches, he might just be able to hold both bells, but there was a good chance he would fall off.

"Can't you go another way?" he asked.

"No," said Crow, who was on tiptoes. "Hurry up!"

Tal grimaced and stretched his leg across. He tested his foothold, then shifted his weight, while keeping hold of the first bell.

He made it, though he was now hanging on to the first bell's wire as much for his own balance as to stop it sounding. It was an awkward position, but he could reach the second bell, though not its wire. Instead, he reached inside and grabbed its clapper.

"Go!" he panted.

Crow jumped again. Tal felt the first wire and the second clapper shiver under his hands.

"Now that one!" called out Crow. But Tal couldn't see him. He was facing the wrong way, and precariously balanced.

"I can't see," called out Tal.

"Dark take it!" swore Crow. "Let go of the first one and swing around."

"I can't!" said Tal. "I'll fall."

"Trust a Chosen to give up!" Crow spat. "I'm only two tiles away! Swing on the clapper of that bell."

"That's easy for you to say!" shouted Tal angrily. He was holding on to the bell's clapper with only three fingers.

Crow didn't answer.

Tal tried to crane his head to see the Freefolk boy, but he couldn't.

Instead, he took a deep breath, let go of the wire, and pushed off from both branches, so that all his weight was on his three fingers and their precarious grip on a single bell clapper.

He swung around, got both legs over a higher

branch and stopped, hanging upside down with his hand still on the clapper, the bell turned up as far as it would go.

"How is this better?" he asked sarcastically.

Crow looked up and laughed a genuine, unexpected laugh. He tried to say something, but the laughter kept getting in the way of the words. He shook so much that he had trouble staying on his tiptoes.

"It's not funny!" shouted Tal.

Crow stopped laughing and wiped his eyes.

"I know," he said, frowning. "I don't know why I laughed. Can you let go of that bell on the count of three, and grab the one across to your left?"

Tal looked at the bell Crow was pointing at. He would have to stay upside down, swing across, and grab the branch with one hand and the bell with the other, all in the time it took Crow to jump.

"I can try," he said. "How will that help?"

If Crow jumped there, he would have to balance on a single red square, on tiptoe, keeping his other foot in the air.

"I can do it," said Crow. "On three, right?"

"Ready," confirmed Tal.

"One. Two... Three!"

He jumped. Tal swung across. Crow's foot came down a fraction of a second before Tal's hand grabbed the wire.

The bell rang once.

Both boys froze, waiting for the other bells to start, or something else to occur. Besides the wire thrumming under Tal's hand, the tree was silent.

"One more and I'll be there," said Crow, his arms stretched out as he balanced precariously, one foot held out behind him. "If I can make it that far."

Tal looked at the tiles Crow would have to jump. There were no white tiles next to the plinth at all. He would have to balance once again on a single red tile. Worse still, Tal wasn't sure which bell went with which tile – the bells were so close together above that point.

He would also have to swing up and there was a branch in between.

"I don't think I can get to the right bell," said Tal worriedly.

Crow tried to look up, but had to stop as he almost overbalanced.

"You'll have to," he said. "I can't stay here like this. On three?"

"No!" Tal called out suddenly. "What if you jump on to the pyramid itself and grab the hands? Would you touch the floor?"

Crow looked across at the plinth. The hands were about level with his neck. It was a long jump, particularly off one foot. But if he could grab the hands, he could hang from them with his feet drawn up, at least till Tal got to the right bell and stilled it.

"I can do that," he said confidently. "Stay where you are."

He crouched on his one foot, toes aching as he kept them pointed. Slowly, he leaned forward, arms quivering to maintain his balance. All his attention was focused on the plinth and the silver hands. He would jump that far and grab them. He would. He must.

It was only when he was already totally committed to the jump that a terrible thought flashed through his mind.

What if the hands weren't securely fixed to the plinth?

26

Finally Milla's voice, hoarse and weary, faltered to a stop. She wet her lips and waited for whatever was going to come next.

"Now we will hear from the Speaking Shadow," announced the Mother Crone. She stamped her foot near the bottle and it rang, metal on metal. The stopper had already been unscrewed.

Odris flowed out in one easy motion, drawing up to her full height next to Milla, overshadowing the Mother Crone. But the old Icecarl woman did not flinch or step away.

"So, Odris, Shadow of the Storm," she said, "you have heard Milla of the Far-Raiders speak. Do you wish to challenge any part of her story?"

"No," said Odris. "Only I want to say that I would be quite happy to give Milla her shadow back, if anyone knows how to do it. Though not if it would kill me or hurt a lot or anything like that," she added hastily. "I mean, I just want to go back to Aenir with Adras."

"You were born after the Forgetting, were you not?" asked the Mother Crone.

Odris nodded.

"Then you cannot be held guilty of making war upon our people," pronounced the Mother Crone.

"Good," said Odris. "Can we go then?"

"No." The Mother Crone walked back behind Milla's chair and spoke to the assembled Crones over the girl's head.

"Milla of the Far-Raiders, by her own voice, is accused of bringing a free shadow to the Ice and of the slaying of the Shield Mother Arla, daughter of Halla, daughter of Luen, daughter of Rucia, daughter of Nuthe, in the line of Grettir since the Ruin of the Ship. You have heard Milla, walked in her dreams, seen from her eyes. What punishment shall be laid upon her, and what shall be done with the shadow that walks at her side?"

No one moved. Then one silver-eyed Crone came forward, taking a dozen slow and somehow threatening steps.

She stood facing Milla. She did not speak.

"In fairness," the Mother Crone announced after a minute or two, "we shall speak with the voice, not the mind."

The Crone looked cross. But she spoke.

"I am Jerrel, sister to Halla, mother of the Shield Mother Arla. Why speak at all, I say? The crimes are clear. She is not fit to go to the Ice. Let her be broken and fed to the Wreska of her clan, and the name... *Milla*... be never borne again by any Icecarl."

Milla closed her eyes. This was almost the worst punishment possible, one of the possibilities she had tried not to think about. If only they would let her go cleanly to the Ice!

Another Crone stepped forward twelve paces, advancing to stand level with, but distant from Jerrel. She was older, her eyes still faintly silver, but the milkiness already swimming in.

"I am Kallim, Clir's daughter, sister of Rucia," she said. "I have heard Milla and walked in her dreams, as I walked in the dying dream of my sister's daughter's daughter Arla. I say that on the slaying, it was an equal combat, not murder, and no punishment is needed. On the bringing of the shadow, it came with Milla, but she did not choose its coming. We must also consider that Milla has done a great service in bringing news of the Chosen's evil and the danger to the Veil. The news could not be brought without the shadow, so on that score I say she is also blameless."

Milla listened in bewilderment. This Crone seemed to be saying that there should be no punishment at all!

No more Crones came out to speak. But after a few minutes, they started to gather behind Jerrel or Kallim, lending support to one or the other.

"They're talking," whispered Odris, who had sidled up next to Milla. "In their heads. I can almost hear it. Like the whispers on the wind."

Milla watched. She had given up all hope, but

now a faint spark had been lit inside her. Maybe there was a chance she would be forgiven, that she could be a Shield Maiden after all...

Only an awful lot of Crones were lining up behind Jerrel, the one who had called for her to be fed to the Wreska. More than were lining up behind Kallim.

After a few minutes there was no further movement of Crones. Milla couldn't be sure, but it looked as if more than half of them were lined up behind Jerrel. If this worked like a normal ship council, then that meant Jerrel would win.

Milla would die ignobly and her name would be permanently blighted.

She shut her eyes, then opened them again as she heard the Crones shuffling.

A third Crone, a full milky-eyed Mother Crone, was striding off to the far end of the room. When she got there she spoke.

"I am the Mother Crone of the Eastern Clans," she said, her voice heavy with power. It made the hair on the back of Milla's neck stand up. "I say that there is a third way to settle the Doom of Milla of the Far-Raiders and the Shadow Odris."

A ripple passed through the assembled ranks of the Crones, slight but enough for Milla to notice.

A third way?

"For her misdeeds, I say she should be cast out of her clan," announced the Mother Crone. "And her name shall be taken from her."

Milla suppressed a sob. *This* was the very worst punishment. Even if she had been fed to the Far-Raiders' Wreska, she would still be one of the clan, and her name, though not to be used again, would be remembered.

To be cast out was to be erased, to have never been an Icecarl at all.

"For her deeds and for the blood she bears," the Mother Crone continued, "let the Outcast then be taken into the Clan of the Ruin Ship and given the name Milla, and confirmed in her ancestry."

Milla choked. How could she be cast out of the Far-Raiders one minute and then adopted by the senior clan of all the Icecarls in the next?

"Further, let this new Milla, Milla of the Ruin Ship, Wielder of the Talon of Danir, be given command of the Expedition we plan," said the Mother Crone of the Eastern Clans. "But as she has trafficked with shadows, let us bind both her and her shadow-companion to the task ahead."

"What Expedition?" asked Milla. "How can I be cast out and then taken in? What... what does it all mean?"

No one answered her. All the Crones were moving across to stand with the Mother Crone of the Eastern Clans.

27

Crow grabbed the silver hands and his knees crashed into the plinth. It hurt, but his feet didn't touch the tiles and the hands did not give way. He hung from them for a moment, then pulled himself up and rested his forearms across the top of the pyramid, on either side of the hands.

Above him, Tal managed to get in a more comfortable and secure position astride a branch that was positioned so he could look straight down at the Keystone.

They both stared at it, Crow from a handsbreadth away, Tal from four or five stretches above.

The Keystone was a large Sunstone, about the

size of a circled thumb and forefinger. It was deeply red and continued to pulse with the slow regularity of a heartbeat.

Crow suddenly craned forward and studied the stone more closely.

"There's... there's someone inside it!" he said. "I can see a woman!"

Tal leaned down lower. He was too far away to see any detail. The stone just looked red to him.

"And there's a shadow with the woman," said Crow. "Smaller than her, some sort of hopping animal... with a long tail."

"It must be the Guardian," said Tal. "Jarnil's cousin Lokar and her Spiritshadow. What's she doing?"

"Just floating, as if the stone is filled with water." Crow shook his head in bewilderment. "And her Spiritshadow just keeps hopping in a circle around her."

"Can you touch the stone?" asked Tal. There had to be some way of getting the Guardian out, or of communicating with her.

Crow nodded and transferred his weight to one

hand. Then he quickly reached across and tapped the stone.

It shifted sideways in the grip of the silver hands and almost fell on to the floor.

A moment later, the Red light grew in intensity and a voice came from the Keystone.

"Who wakes me? Who is there? Speak to me!"

"I am Tal Graile-Rerem," Tal called out. "With me is Crow of the Freefolk."

"Who?" came the voice from the stone. "Rerem's son? And Crow, Bennem's brother?"

"Yes," answered Crow, surprised she knew of his brother.

"Are you Lokar, the Guardian of the Red Keystone?" asked Tal.

"I am," said the woman in the Keystone. "Be quick and focus my Sunstone on the Keystone. Red light in the second intensity will release me."

"Uh, we don't have your Sunstone," Tal replied. "Can I use mine?"

Silence answered him, and a suppressed sob.

"No," Lokar said eventually. "I had hoped you had been sent to release me."

"We would if we could," said Tal. "Where is your Sunstone?"

"I don't know," replied Lokar. "But I used it to unseal the Keystone and it was taken as I did it, so whoever imprisoned me here probably holds it still. Has the Veil... does the Veil... ?"

"It's still working," Tal told her.

A sigh of relief came from the Keystone.

"Then the Empress still guards the secrets of the Violet Keystone," said Lokar. "At the least – perhaps there are other Keystones still sealed. Rerem may know. Was it he who sent you?"

"No," said Tal, his throat suddenly dry. "We think he is trapped like you, inside the Orange Keystone. How... that is... how did you get in there?"

"The Keystones are sealed to the Veil and the Guardians to the Keystones," explained Lokar. "I came here to tune the Keystone, as must be done every year. I unsealed it, but somehow my Sunstone was taken from me as I went within. There was no way back without my own stone and I could not reseal the Keystone from inside."

"Who took your Sunstone?" asked Crow.

"I do not know," replied Lokar. "Someone who could pass the barriers and the bells of the Tower. Someone with ancient knowledge, a true adept of Light magic."

"The Dark Vizier?" asked Tal. "Sushin?"

"Sushin is the Dark Vizier?" asked Lokar, obviously startled. "I did not think... surely the Empress would not appoint someone like him... What is happening in the Castle?"

"There's no time to talk about that," Crow interrupted. "Can I take the Keystone out of here?"

"Yes," said Lokar. "But it needs to be here to power the Veil. It might be lost or destroyed outside the Tower. Leave it here and find my Sunstone."

"I don't take orders from the Chosen," said Crow. He shifted his weight again and reached between the silver hands to take the Keystone.

"No!" shouted Tal. "Leave it!"

Crow ignored him. As he lifted the Keystone free, the silver hands opened, palms up.

Crow lost his balance. Desperately, he clutched at the plinth with his knees and tried to keep hold of the Keystone as well.

He failed. One foot slid down the plinth and pressed hard on a red tile.

Tal saw it about to happen and jumped at the branch that held the appropriate bell. Or what he thought was the right bell. But it was the wrong branch and even as Tal grabbed the wire, another bell sounded only half a stretch away.

The bell jangled discordantly, the sound echoing throughout the room. Then the bell next to it started to sound, and the next. Within a few seconds every bell in the tree was ringing furiously, save the one Tal had in his grip.

He let it go, hung from his hands and jumped down. Crow was already running to the walkway, the Keystone in his hand. Tal followed him. They would have to climb down as quickly as they could, before whatever was alerted by the bell came up the stairs.

Adras had clearly been asleep as they burst out of the archway. The Spiritshadow was lying on the floor of the walkway like a thick blanket of shadow fog and it took him a few seconds to pull himself together.

"What's happening?" he boomed.

Tal ignored him and rushed to the rail, ready to climb over. Crow was already there, but he had stopped and was staring down.

Tal looked.

His heart seemed to stop.

Light was pouring out of every window, stark shafts of light spreading in all directions. It grew brighter as he watched, as Sunstones inside the Tower activated.

It was not the light that scared Tal.

It was the shadows.

Hundreds of Spiritshadows were issuing out of the windows. All kinds of Spiritshadows, all manner of Aeniran beasts. Most of them were creatures Tal had never seen before outside of a game of Beastmaker and they were certainly not companions of Chosen.

Tal couldn't believe his eyes. The Red Tower was housing free shadows, Aeniran creatures that should not have been there, but were.

Now they were all swarming up in answer to the tree of bells.

Tal shouted, "Adras!" ready to order the Spiritshadow to fly them across and away. But the command died on his lips as he saw two Waspwyrm shadows launch themselves out of a window and up.

There would be no escape by flying.

They were trapped.

Everything happened very quickly for Milla once the Crones came to their decision. She was cut free from the chair, but told to say sitting there. Odris was ordered to stand behind her.

Then the Crones quickly moved to form a circle around them both. Milla tried looking out at them, but all the strange eyes focused on her were too much and she had to look down.

When the circle was complete, the Crone Mother of the Ruin Ship slowly raised one scarred, pallid hand.

A wind rose with her hand, though this was unnatural inside the ship. It grew stronger as the hand rose.

A whistling, howling wind circled all around Milla, coming from no single direction. It was strangely cold and hot by turns, unlike any breeze Milla had ever felt upon the Ice.

Milla looked up and saw that the Crones were whistling, their lips pursed, their glowing eyes all centred on her.

Somehow they had called up the wind.

The wind grew stronger, and the lanterns blew out.

The Crones' eyes kept glowing in the darkness.

Then they all spoke together, in a giant voice that was even louder than the wind.

"Milla of the Far-Raiders," roared the collective voice. "For the first time, you are cast out!"

Milla felt the wind pick her up, out of the chair. She was hurled high into the air, above the Crones, almost to the ceiling. Her clothes were stripped from her body and she flew naked through the air.

The wind took her towards the far wall and for a moment Milla thought she would smash into it. At the last moment, the wind dropped and she was hurled through a fur-curtained doorway instead, into a corridor.

Still the wind carried her, and the Crones came in a great mass behind, filling the corridor.

"Milla of the Far-Raiders!" shouted the vast voice again. "For the second time, you are cast out!"

Milla was hurled through another doorway. She felt the wind that carried her meet another, more natural breeze, and for a moment she hovered as the two forces of air did battle. But the Crones' gale was stronger and Milla was pushed on again.

She came to another doorway closed by hung furs. The Ice lay outside, Milla could feel.

"Milla of the Far-Raiders! For the third time, you are cast out!"

The wind cast Milla out through the door and left her. She catapulted through the air and came crashing down into a deep snowdrift.

The shock of the sudden cold knocked the breath out of her. She lay in the snow, the natural wind spraying ice crystals through her hair. Her skin burned with the cold and a deep pain stabbed her through the deep Merwin-horn scar on her stomach.

Her heart seemed to slow down and she felt the blood pumping deep in her ears. It grew slower and slower, but she wasn't frightened or worried. Whatever was happening now, this is what was meant to be. Here, out on the Ice.

Milla's heart stopped.

All was silent. She could no longer hear even the wind.

The silence continued for one second. Two seconds. Three seconds.

Then the Crones spoke again.

"Milla of the Ruin Ship, come to your clan!"

Milla's heart restarted with a shiver she felt from the top of her head to her toes.

Hands delved into the snow and gripped Milla, pulling her from the snow. Her arms were put through a coat of silver Ursek fur – one fit for a Sword-Thane of legend – and it was pulled over her head.

Ice crystals were brushed from her hair and a circlet of Selski bone set there, even as she was momentarily lifted up so her feet could be put into thick boots of fur-lined hide. A belt was tied around her waist, silver and black, with a golden buckle in the shape of a leaping Merwin.

Still dazed, Milla was rushed back inside in the middle of a great crowd of Crones. She felt curiously light, almost as if the wind that had carried her was still doing so. The weight of her past worries had disappeared. She no longer felt that she should go to the Ice and die for her misdeeds.

Back in the judging chamber, Odris rushed to meet her, the Spiritshadow babbling with relief.

"What happened, Milla? I felt you... disappear... and then you were back. I don't like it here. When can we go back to Aenir? It's better there, for both of us..."

"Hush, Odris," said Milla calmly. "We are not finished here. Come stand by me."

She walked to the chair and sat upon it. But in her silver fur and bone circlet, with the Talon of Danir shining on her finger, she did not look like someone come for judgement.

"Welcome, Milla of the Ruin Ship," said the Mother Crone. "We have a heavy responsibility to lay upon you. Do you accept it, for you and your shadow?"

"I do," answered Milla regally. She raised her hand to quiet Odris, who was about to speak.

"Then we shall speak the Prayer of Asteyr to bind you to it," announced the Mother Crone.

Again, the Crones spoke together as a single, giant voice.

A woman's voice.

The power of the voice overwhelmed Milla and Odris, so that after the first few words they did not hear them, but rather felt themselves being caught up in a poem or song, one that reached into their very bones, real and shadow.

With the prayer came a deep instruction, one that they could never break. It spoke of absolute loyalty to the Icecarl people, a loyalty that would be defined by the voice of the Icecarls.

The Crones. They would speak together in their silent way, and make their decisions in the great mind they shared. Whatever decisions they made would be laid upon Milla and she must obey, as must the shadow that was bound to her.

The Prayer changed and the voice grew quieter. Finally only the Mother Crone of the Ruin Ship spoke. Even alone, her voice was binding.

"Three things we lay upon you," said the Mother Crone. "The first is your life-name, so I call you Milla Talon-Hand. The second is the office I have held before you, that of the Living Sword of Asteyr. The third is a title and a responsibility that no Icecarl has borne for two thousand circlings."

She paused and took a deep breath before continuing.

"Milla Talon-Hand, we name you War-Chief of the Icecarls and charge you to finish what was begun long ago. We charge you to secure our world forever from the Shadows of Aenir."

Tal looked at the great tide of Spiritshadows rising towards them. They only had a few minutes before they would swarm over him.

He looked at Crow, but the older boy was paralysed, staring down at their enemies, the Red Keystone loose in his hand.

Tal saw it and had a sudden thought.

He acted quickly, snatching the Keystone from Crow's slack grip.

Instantly, Crow turned, his knife in his hand.

"Give it back!" he snarled.

"What's happening?" came a plaintive voice from the Keystone, as Tal backed away.

"I need it to get us out of here," Tal explained, speaking as fast as he could. "Unless you want to meet those Spiritshadows?"

Crow hesitated, then lowered his knife.

Tal stared at the Keystone. He could see Lokar, suspended in Red light. She looked like she was treading water. Obviously it took some effort to make contact with the outside world.

"Lokar," he said urgently, "there are heaps of Spiritshadows coming up the outside of the Tower. Is there anywhere here we can hide, that will be safe from them? Can they come through the arches?"

"Yes, if they have been given the Words," said Lokar, frowning in thought. "You will not be safe here. What is your Spiritshadow? Can it fly?"

"A Storm Shepherd, so yes, but there are flying shadows, so we will be pursued." Tal looked up at Crow, who was still standing there, watching him suspiciously. "Crow! Keep watch. Tell me when they're about fifty stretches away!"

Crow reluctantly went to look over the side.

"You look young," said Lokar. "Have you mastery of the seven colours?"

"Not exactly mastery," replied Tal. "But I can do things... I've done things..."

"Ninety stretches," shouted Crow. "There are hundreds of them!"

"Can you combine all seven?" asked Lokar.

"Yes," said Tal, almost before Lokar had stopped speaking.

"Then you can make a miniature dark veil to hide beneath," said Lokar. "Find a corner, crouch in it and I will tell you how to weave a veil. Quickly!"

Tal looked around widely.

"Fifty stretches!" shouted Crow. He looked at Tal, wide-eyed and clearly frightened. "Whatever you're going to do, do it quickly."

"Let's fight!" boomed Adras. He leaned over the railing and fired off a bolt of shadow-lightning. A sudden, ghastly squeal announced that it had found its mark.

"No, Adras!" shouted Tal. He went to the wall and tugged at a downpipe that carried rainwater from the dome high above. "Help me pull this off!"

The downpipe was set into a recess in the wall. If they could crouch down there and weave a veil, there was a chance the Spiritshadows wouldn't be able to find them.

Crow didn't know what he planned, but he rushed to Tal's side and pulled at the pipe too. It gave a little, but it wasn't until Adras reached above them both and tugged that it tore away with the screech of metal on stone.

"Quick!" instructed Tal. "Crouch down here, as close as we can get!"

He pushed into the recess with Crow. Adras made himself as thin as possible and slid in behind Tal and up the wall.

"What now?" said Crow.

Tal didn't answer. He was looking at the Keystone, watching Lokar and focusing on his own Sunstone at the same time.

Crow and Adras watched the railing, expecting to see a Spiritshadow leap over and attack at any moment.

"Hurry up!" Crow murmured. Tendrils of differently-coloured light were starting to rise out of Tal's Sunstone, but very slowly.

The tendrils issued out and wove together in

front of the pressed-in trio. As they wove together, a patch of darkness formed in the air. It spread rapidly, curving up, down and around.

"Faster," whispered Crow. He saw a taloned shadow-hand grip the railing, behind the forming veil. "Faster!"

A Spiritshadow leapt over the railing – a huge Waspwyrm, shadow-wings still beating, sting looking all too solid in the Red light.

Crow saw it and he stopped breathing as its head slowly swivelled in his direction. The veil was almost blocking his view. It would be so close. Would the Spiritshadow look first or would the veil be formed in time?

The miniature veil spread across and seamlessly joined to form a perfect sphere around them, a fraction of a second before the Spiritshadow turned its head.

Crow shivered and was startled to find he needed to take a very deep breath.

"Don't do that," said Tal sharply.

"What?" Crow asked softly. He wasn't sure if sound travelled through the veil.

"It's fine to talk," said Tal. He touched the veil, and his finger rebounded as if the veil were tightly stretched cloth. "Just don't breathe too much."

"Why?" asked Crow.

"I was in a hurry—" Tal started to explain.

"What?" asked Crow.

"I made it too solid," said Tal. "I don't think there's any air getting through."

"What?" Crow gasped. He reached out and his fingernails scraped down the veil.

It was solid.

"We have to get out," Crow whispered. "We'll die in here."

"There's enough air for a while," said Tal. He was fighting to stay calm. Just knowing that their air was running out was making him feel terrible. Weak and pathetic. "We have to be still."

Crow looked at him, panic in his eyes. He raised his hand and Tal cringed, thinking he was going to punch him. Then Crow pulled back.

"Sorry," he said. "I'll… I'll be still."

They sat in silence for a while, then Crow suddenly looked at Tal.

"Where's Adras?" he asked, craning his head around.

There was no sign of the Spiritshadow.

All the colour drained from Tal's face. No wonder he felt so terrible.

"He must be outside! They're killing him!"

"No, he isn't!" said a small voice from the Keystone. Tal hurriedly peered down at it.

"He's in your veil!" exclaimed Lokar. "You wove him into it and he has no light!"

"No air for us, no light for Adras," muttered Crow.

"It's better than getting killed by Spiritshadows!" Tal retorted. "Besides, we only have to wait till they're gone."

"We might be dead by then," said Crow. "How will we know when they do go anyway?"

Lokar said something both boys missed. They leaned down at the same time to hear better and cracked their heads.

"Dark!" swore Crow. He snatched the Keystone back and said, "Be more careful!"

Tal raised his Sunstone for a second, then thought better of it. He didn't want Crow to have the Keystone, but there wasn't much he could do about it now.

"What was that?" Crow asked Lokar.

Tal leaned forward again, more carefully.

"You both need to save your breath," said Lokar. "As far as I can tell from in here, Tal has made this veil too well."

"What do you mean?" asked Tal.

"Not only is it too solid," said Lokar. "I doubt that you can unthread it. You'll have to wait till it frays of its own accord."

Tal and Crow looked at each other. Words seemed at the tips of their tongues, but neither spoke. Instead they settled back and exhaled slowly at the same time.

I wish I'd learned Milla's Rovkir breathing, thought Tal, as the minutes slowly passed, marked by the spark of his Sunstone. It was getting warmer and stuffier, and it seemed to him that Crow was using up too much of their air.

He glanced across and saw Crow's eyes glittering. His hand was on his knife. Clearly he had the same thought. There might only be enough air for one of them to survive.

One must die for the other to live.

Crow pulled his knife out an inch.

Tal raised his Sunstone though it felt like a great weight and shook his head.

Crow eased the knife back in. Tal lowered his hand.

Both kept watching each other, alert for the slightest movement.

At least Tal thought he was alert. But he suddenly realised his head was on his chest. He snapped it up, only to see Crow's head lolling sideways.

The Freefolk boy seemed to be unconscious.

For a moment Tal was tempted to finish him off, so he would have more air. But only for a moment. What was it his great-uncle had said to him?

"Do not be a caveroach."

It would be a caveroach thing to do, to kill Crow for a few breaths that might not be enough anyway.

Instead, Tal feebly pressed at the dark veil. As before, his fingers bounced off it. It seemed as strong as ever and he could feel Adras trapped inside. Fading with every moment.

Tal took a shallow breath and closed his eyes.

It was much easier just to go to sleep.

As Tal's eyes closed, Crow's opened. He touched his knife once… twice… then slowly closed his eyes again.

Tal awoke in sudden panic, Red light on his face, fresh air in his nostrils and a terrible headache throbbing above his eyes. Crow was stirring at his side, but there was no sign of Adras.

Or of the enemy Spiritshadows.

Tal looked at his Sunstone. Over an hour had passed. They were very lucky the veil had unravelled when it did. Judging by how terrible he felt, another few minutes would probably have asphyxiated them.

A low groan came from the other side of Crow. Tal crawled over and stared aghast at the tiny, shrivelled shadow which was all that remained of Adras.

"Light!" whimpered the mere dab of darkness that was about the size of Tal's foot. "Light!"

There was plenty of Red light around, but Tal

lowered his Sunstone, shielded it with his hand and directed a bright beam of light matched to the colour of Aenir's sun upon his stricken Spiritshadow.

Slowly, the shadow thickened and began to spread out across the stones. As it grew, Tal's headache lessened.

He was so intent upon revitalising Adras that he didn't notice Crow had recovered too, until the Freefolk boy was standing next to him. He had the Keystone raised almost to his chin and was whispering to it.

"Lokar says there is a secret stair that starts two levels below," he said to Tal. Obviously he had decided to ignore what had gone on inside the miniature veil. "If we can climb down to it, she can guide us through the traps. It comes out..."

He listened to the Keystone again and continued, "It comes out in a White Corridor, between Red One and Orange Seven. It shouldn't be too hard to get from there to an Underfolk store and then back to my domain."

Tal nodded, though he secretly flinched at Crow

calling any part of the Castle "his domain". If there was anything he had learned since his fall to the world outside, it was the importance of keeping his mouth shut – until the time was right.

"Weak," said Adras. He had regained his usual form, but his shadowflesh was almost transparent, barely visible.

"He will be slow to recover," said Crow, repeating Lokar's words. "You must give him light for as long as you can, and lots of it before we go through the Veil proper."

Tal nodded.

"Where are the Spiritshadows?" he asked. "Can you see any?"

"I guess they've gone back into their hideyholes," said Crow. "At least I couldn't see any when I looked over the side."

"They're there somewhere," said Tal. "Hiding. Waiting. I would like to know what for."

Crow shrugged. That was a problem for another time. He had what he'd come for. He tucked the Keystone carefully into a slim leather pouch he wore on a chain around his neck.

"Come on," he said, as he carefully climbed over the railing. "Stay close. You might need to make another veil. But we'd better be able to breathe in the next one."

Tal watched Crow go over. He was more suspicious than ever about Crow. It was clear the Freefolk boy only wanted him around for what he could do. Crow hated the Chosen so much that he wouldn't hesitate to get rid of Tal if he thought he was of no more use.

The worst thing about it, Tal thought sadly, was that he couldn't really blame Crow. He had a lot to hate the Chosen for.

"Adras," he said, raising his hand, "wrap around my Sunstone and arm, and get as much light as you can."

Adras nodded, too weak to boom a reply. Tal felt him move on to his arm, a cool touch that made the hair on his skin prickle with small lightning bolts. His Sunstone dimmed as Adras covered it, though the light still blazed under the shadow.

Tal climbed over the railing and gingerly felt for a foothold.

31

Milla stood in the Hall of the Reckoner, the Mother Crone at her side. Both looked down at the complex puzzle of hundreds of tiles and models that depicted the entire world of the Ice and the Icecarl clan-ships that moved upon it. Shield Maiden cadets moved across the huge map, moving the ship models and, less frequently, exchanging the tiles that told of the quality and condition of the Ice. Seven Crones, seated on tall chairs of woven bone, directed the cadets.

When Milla had last seen the Reckoner, the clan-ships of the Icecarls had been spread all over the world, in no apparent pattern. Now there were clumps of ships forming at various parts of the maps. As Milla watched, a Crone summoned a Shield Maiden cadet and spoke to her. The young girl listened, then stepped lightly across the tiles to one of the gatherings of ships and selected one of the smallest, that had a Sunstone chip set in its prow. This ship she picked up and moved to an adjacent tile.

Milla noticed it was moving towards the tile at the centre of the Reckoner, a tile that had the model of a mountain upon it and a miniature Ruin Ship at its side.

"Yes," said the Mother Crone. "The clans are gathering where they may, and one ship in every seven is bringing all the Shield Maidens and hunters the clans can spare from following the Selski. We have summoned the Sword-Thanes too, though they do not appear upon the Reckoner, and we cannot know how many will be able to answer the call – or will choose to."

Milla nodded. It was all a bit much for her. She had been cast out, reborn as Milla Talon-Hand and named War-Chief only that morning. Now everyone expected her to take charge and do whatever had to be done to take over the Castle, force the Chosen to give up their Spiritshadows and then to... she didn't know what... cross over to Aenir and do the Forgetting all over again?

"The ships will come as quickly as they can," the Mother Crone was saying. "Yet it will be many sleeps before the full host is gathered. Is it your wish, War-Chief, that the Shield Maidens and hunters we have here be gathered for an initial attack upon the Castle, to secure the passage into it?"

"Um, yes," Milla replied.

The Mother Crone smiled, a smile so brief Milla nearly missed it. The Crone wasn't really asking her, Milla realised. She was helping her work out what to do, but making it look like she was in charge of the military detail. Though everyone knew both she and Odris had to do what the Crones told them.

"Yes," Milla said more firmly. "Let them prepare. I will lead them out after the main sleep. I need... I need to rest a little."

"They will be ready," answered the Mother

Crone. "Before you go to rest, War-Chief, I would have you meet Malen. She is the youngest of the Crones and so best suited for the arduous task of accompanying you on this first attack."

Before the Mother Crone finished speaking, a young Crone stepped through the curtains of the door and approached. She was young, Milla saw. Blue-eyed, as all beginning Crones were, with a luminosity in the blue. But she didn't look much older than sixteen circlings, hardly older than Milla. She felt a stab of jealousy in her heart. This Icecarl girl had found her place without trouble, Milla thought. She was not constrained by the Prayer of Asteyr, an untrustworthy but necessary evil the Icecarls were prepared to put up with due only to the greater danger that threatened them.

"I greet you, War-Chief Milla Talon-Hand," said Malen. She clubbed her fists together, as did Milla.

Even her voice was perfect, thought Milla. She had a clear, bell-like voice, perfect for singing or chanting the old epics. Everyone must have loved her in her clan, and now they would be so proud of her, a Crone at so young an age.

"I will come with you as the Voice of the Crones," said Malen.

Milla nodded. That was even worse. When Malen wanted to, she could speak with the authority of all the Crones and Milla, bound by the Prayer, would have to do what she said.

Unless she told Milla, Milla wouldn't know if Malen wasn't connecting with the other Crones, or speaking only for herself.

For a moment Milla considered asking the Mother Crone if someone else, someone older and more experienced, could come with her as the Voice of the Crones. But she didn't.

"We leave immediately after main sleep," said Milla briskly. "I must rest now. Come, Odris."

All the Shield Maiden cadets in the room clubbed their fists as Milla left, but she noticed many seemed reluctant to do so. The Crones had made her War-Chief, but it was not as easy as that. She would have to earn the respect of the cadets and the Shield Maidens and the hunters and Sword-Thanes who would come.

She would also have to work out how to get

through the bad air of the heatways, counter Chosen Sunstone magic and secure the way from Mountain to Castle in order to bring in reinforcements once she had established a foothold in the Underfolk levels. Then there were the Underfolk themselves to consider, and the likelihood of Ebbitt, Jarnil and the Freefolk aiding the Icecarls or turning against them.

And there was Tal. Milla wondered what he was doing and whether he had been successful in gaining the Keystone. She wasn't sure if she wanted him to succeed or fail. If Tal did get the Keystone and somehow managed to turn the Chosen against Sushin and the free shadows, he might be able to secure the Veil. But knowing him as she did, she was sure he would not want to send all the Chosen's Spiritshadows back to Aenir.

So he would be an enemy and there was only one absolutely sure way to deal with an enemy.

Kill them before they killed you.

32

The climb down was nerve-racking. Both Tal and Crow expected to meet hostile Spiritshadows at any moment. Every flicker of light startled them – and sometimes that was enough to make them almost slip or lose their grip. Then they would have another pang of fear as they nearly fell off.

But no Spiritshadows came out of the Tower, and they made it safely down to the window that Lokar had described to Crow. Climbing through that, they found the secret stair. It was a very narrow stairway, hidden within the thick wall of the Tower. Anyone much larger than Crow could easily get stuck.

There were also frequent traps. Crow had to take the Keystone out of his pouch and hold it close to his ear, listening to Lokar's instructions as he kept up a running commentary to describe to her where they were.

The worst trap was where a rack of razor-edged cleavers swung out across the stairway. The cleavers were positioned at knee, stomach and neck height, Lokar said. The trap was triggered by treading anywhere but the very centre of each of six steps. With every one Tal expected to trip, to hear the "snick" of the mechanism and then feel the sudden bite of the cleavers.

Somehow he made it through.

Tal followed Crow closely, not trusting the Freefolk boy to tell him about the traps. He figured if he stayed close he would be safe.

Adras was still wrapped around his arm and Sunstone, absorbing light. His shadowflesh was slowly darkening, but he had been very close to death. Tal didn't want to think what would happen to him if his Spiritshadow died.

The Veil looked strange when they came to it. It

cut through the walls of the Tower as if they weren't there. It looked like the stair descended into a pool of the inkiest, darkest water.

Crow hesitated at the Veil and listened to Lokar, the Keystone held to his ear. Then he plunged straight down, his hand tracing the wall.

Tal paused too, and concentrated on his Sunstone, releasing a burst of incredibly bright and powerful light. Adras absorbed it and only a dull glow spread out from Tal's hand.

"Are you ready for the Veil?" Tal asked.

"Yes," whispered Adras. "Go quickly!"

Tal took a deep breath, reached out to touch the wall himself and stepped down.

One step, two steps, three steps... and the Veil closed over his face.

Tal was in total darkness. He kept on stepping down, grazing his fingers as he pushed hard against the wall, reassuring himself that it was there.

Ten steps... eleven steps... twelve steps... panic started to rise in Tal. The Veil seemed thicker here. Surely it was taking longer than before. This should be easier than climbing through it.

He took the stairs more quickly, almost falling in his eagerness to get through. He lost count of the steps and began to take them two at a time.

He had to get out of the Veil!

Suddenly he was out. Crow looked up at him from further down the narrow, winding stair, the Red Keystone glowing in his hand.

Tal swallowed and slowly stood upright. He'd hunched down to an almost animal posture in his desperation to get lower, to get through the Veil.

"Are you all right?" he asked Adras. The Spiritshadow was still wound around his arm and wasn't moving.

"Yes," came the weak reply. "Sick. Light is good."

"Let's go," called Crow. He was clearly in a hurry.

At the base of the stair, where a secret panel opened out into a colourless corridor, they had to wait for a pair of Spiritshadows to pass. With the panel open a crack, Tal and Crow watched them disappear around the corner.

One was a Klenten Warbeast. It had a massive head armoured with flanges of thick bone, set upon immense shoulders. It ran as often on four legs as two. The other was a Dretch, the stick-insect-and-spider combination, like his cousins'. But this Spiritshadow was larger and its shadowflesh was stronger and more defined.

Tal bit his lip with worry. All the Spiritshadows in the Castle should be with their Chosen. These two were free shadows, like the ones in the Red Tower. How many Aenirans were already roaming around the Castle while the Chosen were in Aenir? They were confident enough to simply walk the corridors. They didn't expect to meet any opposition.

"I think Sushin must be very close to destroying the Veil," Tal whispered to Crow. "There are so many Spiritshadows already here. We need to talk to Lokar about this as soon as we get somewhere safe."

"Maybe," replied Crow. He seemed distracted. "Look, there's another one!"

Tal bent to look through the gap. The next thing he felt was a terrible shock to the back of his head and an intense pain.

Dimly he realised that Crow had hit him with the

hilt of his knife. He tried to get up, but there was no strength in his muscles. He couldn't see properly either. Everything was blurry and the walls and floor were swaying.

"Nothing personal, Tal," said Crow, his voice coming from high up and far away. "If you weren't a Chosen, you'd be all right. But you are a Chosen, and I've got things to do with this Keystone that you wouldn't agree with."

Tal groaned. He could feel Adras struggling to form himself and attack Crow, but the Spiritshadow was still too weak.

A glint of steel caught Tal's eye and a terrible jolt of fear shot through him.

"No," he tried to say as Crow bent down next to him, his knife in his hand.

"Your people killed my parents and drove my brother crazy," whispered Crow. "My grandparents went into the Hall of Nightmares too, and were never the same. It is... justice... to kill any Chosen."

Despite his words, Crow did not make any move with the knife. He just sat there, looking at Tal.

Their gaze met. Tal couldn't see or think

properly, but it wasn't hate he saw in Crow's eyes. It was fear, though there was nothing for Crow to fear here.

Except himself. The Freefolk boy looked away from Tal, towards the knife in his hand. The steel glittered, red in the light from the Keystone.

"Sorry," Crow said abruptly. "Don't come after me."

He stood up, looked through the gap again, then slipped out into the corridor.

Tal groaned and felt his head. There was no blood, but it hurt a lot. Pushing against the floor with his hands, he managed to stagger upright.

Adras tried to help him, but there was no strength in his body. Chosen and Spiritshadow leaned together and fell against the wall.

"What do we do now?" Adras asked plaintively.

"We get the Keystone back," said Tal grimly. Using the wall as a prop, he edged to the panel and looked out. Crow was just disappearing around a corner opposite the one the Spiritshadows had taken.

"Come on," he said, pushing himself off with an effort. He was still dizzy, but he could walk. Crow was not going to get away with the Keystone that easily.

Crow was gone by the time Tal managed to get to the corner. The corridor stretched into the distance, the bright white light of the Sunstones set in its ceiling painful to Tal's damaged head. There were lots of corridors joining it, leading off into Red One or Orange Seven.

But Crow wouldn't have taken those, Tal knew. He would head straight for the closest Underfolk store or service-way.

Still stumbling, Adras hooked on to his belt like a blind follower, Tal wove his way down the corridor. He was kept going by the fury that burned inside him. How dare Crow hit him! It was a coward's hit too. At least Milla had always hit him face-to-face.

He flung open the first Underfolk door he came to, Sunstone ring raised, already burning with Red light. But this was only a long closet full of spare robes, cleaning equipment and the like.

Tal was about to back out when his eyes caught the flash of something behind the robes hanging at the back. A faint glimpse of some Red light, only for an instant. The Red light of the Keystone.

He rushed over and pulled the robes away in a frenzy. There was a door behind them, now closed. It had no handle or obvious means of opening.

Tal didn't look for one. He raised his hand and focused his rage upon his Sunstone. Red light answered, a thick, burning ray that flashed out at the door.

Tal retreated as liquid metal flew. He clenched his fist, ring outward, and directed the beam in a wide circle.

In a moment, he had cut the metal door in half. Whatever lock it had once had was now melted into a blob. Tal picked up a mop handle and used it to smash the remnants of the smoking door aside before going through.

A small room lay beyond, and a familiar, larger metal door, locked by a wheel. It was an entryway to the steam pipes of the Castle. A few stretches away on the same wall was another narrow stairway, an inspection-way for the steam system.

Crow was at the top of the stairs. He turned as he saw Tal.

"I told you not to follow me!"

"Give me the Keystone!" ordered Tal. He kept his Sunstone raised. The red glare of it was a clear warning.

"No," said Crow. "The Freefolk need it."

"Why?" asked Tal. "Why bash me in the head? I might have agreed with you."

Crow let out a short, bitter laugh. "A Chosen agree with what I plan! Listen, Tal. I've had a Sunstone for five years. I got it off... well, I got it. But no one will teach me how to use it properly. Sure, Jarnil's showed me a few tricks, and your great-uncle Ebbitt. But they're afraid. Afraid to let a Freefolk into their secrets. But now I've got Lokar and she'll teach me anything, just so long as I talk to her. It's lonely inside that stone. Nothing ever happens. You can go crazy in there."

"That's it?" asked Tal. He couldn't believe it was so simple. "I'd teach you, if you want."

"No, that's not it!" Crow screamed. "We've got quite a few Sunstones hidden away. Once we know how to use them, the Fatalists will join us. We'll use the Sunstones to overcome the Spiritshadows who guard the most important Chosen while they're in Aenir. Once we have the bodies as hostages we can *tell* the Chosen what to do."

"But what about Sushin and the Veil?" said Tal. "Crow, our whole *world* is in danger! This isn't the time to fight among ourselves."

"It's never the time if you listen to the Chosen," Crow whispered, almost to himself. His knife flashed in his hand and then it was in the air, flying straight at Tal.

It struck the wall behind him in a shower of sparks.

Instinctively, Tal fired back a Red Ray of Destruction.

Crow ducked as the ray cut across the stone

above his head, sending chips flying. One cut the Freefolk boy across the face, leaving a trail of blood across his cheek.

Crow cried out and charged at Tal. At the same time, Adras leapt forward. He wasn't strong enough to do much, but he put out one puffy foot and Crow catapulted over it.

Unfortunately, he went straight into Tal.

The two boys rolled around on the ground, punching and kicking. Adras managed to get one shadow-arm around Crow's neck long enough to pull him off. As they split apart, Tal snatched the pouch that held the Red Keystone.

Adras couldn't hold Crow. He flung the Spiritshadow off and snatched up his knife.

The two boys faced each other across the room. Adras retreated to stand next to Tal.

"Don't make me hurt you any more," said Crow. "Give me the Keystone."

"No," said Tal. He raised his Sunstone. It swirled with Orange light now, for Tal had a different plan. His anger had cooled. He didn't want to kill Crow. He would use Orange light to push the boy away.

Crow started to raise his knife.

Tal prepared a massive blast.

For a long moment, there was the faint possibility that both of them would back down.

Then Tal heard voices coming up the stairs behind Crow. Freefolk voices. Crow must have arranged this place as a rendezvous, must have planned to backstab Tal.

Tal let the blast of Orange light go, aiming just above Crow's head.

Crow heard the voices too, but the one his ears picked out was Tal's great-uncle Ebbitt. Ebbitt was a Chosen Adept, and his Spiritshadow was fierce and strong. He would take Tal's side if he knew what was really going on.

Crow threw his knife.

Clovil was at the top of the stairs, with Ferek, Inkie and Ebbitt close behind. Ebbitt saw Crow's back and he called out to him, just as the blast of Orange light struck directly above them all.

The blast knocked the Freefolk boy back, but that wasn't all. At the same time it cracked the great beams of the roof and the lintel above the door. Rock shattered and began to pour down, at first in tiny pebbles, then quickly becoming a great cascade of crushing stones.

Tal saw it all happen. He saw Crow catapulted back into Clovil. He saw the other Freefolk look up in sudden fear as the roof caved in, and he heard his great-uncle's surprised shout.

"Back! Back for your lives!"

Then the stairway was completely buried in a flood of falling stones. A huge piece of the ceiling fell in front of Tal, shattering into tiny pieces that flew up and cut his face and hands. More rock fell, and dust billowed out in huge clouds.

Despite the danger, Tal rushed forward. He concentrated on his Sunstone to make a Hand of Light to try and shift the great weight of stone.

But even as the Hand formed, a sudden, terrible whistle sounded above and in front of him. Instinctively, Tal ducked, a moment before a great gout of steam exploded out above his head.

The steam pipe had cracked! It was the huge riser that carried vast quantities of steam up from the lava-heated pools deep below.

Desperately Tal focused, to create the Hand before the superhot steam found its way through the cracks.

The whistle grew even fiercer and more shrill as steam howled out under great pressure. The heat was unbearable and Tal was forced to crawl back.

He lost concentration and the beginning of the Hand of Light winked out.

Pushed back by the steam, Tal had to retreat into the Underfolk's store. He couldn't see anything now. The room beyond was completely full of steam and dust. Deep inside the killing cloud Tal could hear rocks still falling, with a boom that vibrated through the floor.

"Help!" Tal screamed. He didn't care who came. There had to be somebody who could so something. "Help!"

He tried to enter the room again, but was beaten back. Even at the edges the steam was too hot to bear. Further in, it would strip the flesh from bones.

Coughing, Tal retreated again and screamed once more for help.

But no help came. The Chosen were all in Aenir, and the Underfolk would not look in here until they were sure they were supposed to do so.

Tal couldn't do anything. Adras couldn't do anything.

Tal couldn't believe what had happened.

He had probably *killed* Crow, Clovil, Ferek, Inkie... and Great-Uncle Ebbitt.

All in one fatal second.

He hadn't meant to, but it had happened. Even if by some chance they had ducked the falling rock, they couldn't have lived through the explosion of steam.

Adras plucked at his sleeve.

Tal looked down and dumbly saw that Crow's knife was caught in a fold of cloth under his arm. It hadn't pierced the skin, but it had missed his heart by less than a handspan.

"What do we do now?" asked Adras, his voice small, not at all like a Storm Shepherd's. "I wish Odris was here."

Tal stared from side to side. He couldn't think. He didn't know what to do.

A tiny voice coming from the bag he held in his fist finally caught his attention.

"What's going on?"

Tal pulled out the Red Keystone and looked into it. A tear splashed on the stone. Tal wiped it away. He hadn't known he was crying.

"What is it?" asked Lokar. "What's happening?"

"Crow's dead," said Tal woodenly. He didn't mention the others.

"Never mind that," said Lokar. "He was only an Underfolk, and crazy. You must take me to the Empress. It is absolutely the most important thing. Life or death!"

"Life or death," repeated Tal. He felt like someone else was using his voice.

"The only question is how to get to her without going through the Dark Vizier... or the light for that matter," mused Lokar. "Tal – are you listening?"

"Yes," Tal mumbled. He couldn't think for himself. He was too deep in shock.

"What is that date? Are we close to any of the Festivals, or anything the Empress would appear at?"

"It's the Day of Ascension," said Tal. "Or the day after. I don't know..."

"Aenir!" cried Lokar. "The Empress will be in Aenir. You must take me there, Tal!"

"I've killed—" Tal started to cry out, but Lokar interrupted him.

"Aenir! The Empress. She will sort everything

out. She can release Rerem using the Violet Keystone!"

That got Tal's attention. Releasing his father. He had to talk to his father about what had happened.

"Aenir," he mumbled. He would have to find somewhere safe to hide his body, because he couldn't leave Adras behind to guard it. Adras couldn't be trusted to stay on the job.

"The Mausoleum," he whispered. He looked back into the swirling mass of steam and stone dust one last time. Sweat poured off his face, mingling with tears.

"We'll cross to Aenir from the Mausoleum," he decided aloud.

"Aenir?" asked Adras, as Tal began to run, run away from the terrible place behind him. "What about Odris and Milla?"

Tal didn't answer. He kept running.

"We should wait," the Spiritshadow pleaded. "Odris is coming, with Milla. I can feel it!"

Tal didn't hear him. There was only one thing on his mind.

He had to cross over to Aenir. He must do what

he had wanted to do all along.

Tell the Empress everything.

Then *everything* would be her problem.

EPILOGUE

Three days after the rock fall in the Castle, but far below on the Mountain of Light, Milla Talon-Hand watched the rope bridge being thrown over the gap in the road. All around her, more than forty Shield Maidens laboured, hammering in supports and tying ropes. There were more on the other side, near the pyramid of Imrir, doing the same job. Others stood by with moth-lanterns to light the work, or with spears, to guard against Perawls.

Two Sword-Thanes stood below the heatway entrance, guarding against whatever might come from above or below. They both had great bows of bent bone in their hands, and quivers full of bone arrows fletched with the feathers of the blind Arug bird.

Malen the Crone stood with the Sword-Thanes, her luminous blue eyes intent upon the darkness beyond the Icecarls' lights. What she looked for, Milla did not know.

Soon, provided the Crones could supply them with clean air, her first raiding force would begin the journey through the heatways.

And Milla would lead them.